"Cliff," Melanie managed, taking a breath for courage, "do you mind if I ask you a personal question?"

"Shoot." He squinted up through the sun, his hair matted from the work.

You're so helpful and good-looking I want to pinch myself. I would like you to wrap your arms around me. Do you like me? Do you think you could learn to like me? Would you ever marry me and take me away from here?

"You were saying?" the boy asked.

"Nothing."

"What?"

"Oh nothing, it's all right," she said, suddenly feeling hopeless. "Really."

Melanie thanked Cliff and watched as he gave Nina another glance before he jumped back into his car and headed through the post entrance.

"What happened to you?" Nina said, shaking her head as Melanie drove them home. "You were supposed to give him your phone number, not the agriculture report on Castroville."

"What was the point? He's going to be tied up for eight weeks."

"There's always afterward."

"He was more interested in you," Melanie said.

"I've got a boyfriend. We weren't here for me."

"He wasn't my type anyway."

"Excuses," said Nina. "Whatever happened to Melanie the Fearless?"

Other Bantam Starfire Books you will enjoy

SOLDIER BOY

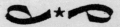

Michael French

BANTAM BOOKS
NEW YORK · TORONTO · LONDON · SYDNEY · AUCKLAND

SOLDIER BOY

A Bantam Book / published by arrangement with
the author

PRINTING HISTORY
First published by The Putnam and Grosset Group 1985

Bantam edition / November 1990

The Starfire logo is a registered trademark of Bantam Books,
a division of Bantam Doubleday Dell Publishing Group, Inc.
Registered in U.S. Patent and Trademark Office and elsewhere.

ISBN 0-553-28609-9

Published simultaneously in the United States and Canada

Bantam Books are published by Bantam Books, a division of Bantam Doubleday Dell Publishing Group, Inc. Its trademark, consisting of the words "Bantam Books" and the portrayal of a rooster, is Registered in U.S. Patent and
Trademark Office and in other countries. Marca Registrada. Bantam Books,
666 Fifth Avenue, New York, New York 10103.

PRINTED IN THE UNITED STATES OF AMERICA

10 9 8 7 6 5 4 3 2 1

For Dennis,
brother, leader, friend

SOLDIER BOY

1

"**H**ow do I look? Do I look okay?" Melanie asked her friend Nina, ignoring the steering wheel to peek in the rearview mirror. Her freckled face with its pug nose and big eyes sometimes reminded her of Little Orphan Annie. Disaster, Melanie thought. Makeup helped a little. She was not *un*pretty, she finally judged herself, but she was forever searching for ways to be prett*ier*.

"You really think this is going to work?" Nina said, as the beat-up convertible passed the spring tourists. The rugged coastline of Monterey Bay shimmered under the brilliant sky. "It's a cornball idea."

"Cornball to you, maybe. I think it's a thrilling adventure."

"Adventure, sure," Nina deadpanned.

"Here we are," Melanie announced as she squealed to a stop on the highway shoulder. It was exactly one minute before five. Right on time, Melanie thought. A brown metal sign arched across the six-lane entrance to Fort Ord and proclaimed HOME OF THE 7th U.S. INFANTRY DIVISION. It was also a basic training headquarters, Melanie knew, with fifty times more young men than the small, hokey town she was stranded in a few miles away. As going-home traffic streamed through the post gates, the MP on duty delivered a crisp salute to the officers while enlisted men earned only his sullen stare. Behind the miles of barbed-wire fence, Melanie spotted the PX, the post movie theater, the commissary, rifle ranges, and endless rows of sea-green barracks that housed the basic training companies. That much she knew from a map. She had never been inside the small, forbidden city, which made it all the more intriguing.

"Let's get this over with," Nina said. "I have to get home to study."

"Hey, honor student, it's Friday, the weekend, remember? Even you can relax." Melanie was about to throw up her hands at her friend. "You're really something, Nina. I don't think you know how to have fun." Melanie quickly crouched by the Chevy's rear tire—the one that was visible from the highway—and let the air out. As they'd rehearsed, Nina opened the trunk, removed the jack and spare tire, and in view of the Fort Ord traffic propped the jack upside down under the car. Both girls stared helplessly at the flat.

"So why isn't anybody stopping?" Nina said after a minute, trying not to laugh.

"Face the road more. You're the one who's better-looking."

"I can't. It's like we're desperate."

"*I'm* not desperate," Melanie corrected. "I'm determined. Haven't you heard of the liberated woman?"

"A liberated woman can change her own tire," Nina said loftily. "I just can't do this."

"You better," Melanie threatened. "Best friends aren't supposed to cop out."

Resigned, Nina tossed a hand through her fine blonde hair just as an ocean breeze caught her lacy dress and made it billow like a parachute. A passing car rolled to a stop.

Immediately Melanie decided that there were only two problems. The first was that the car was going *into* Fort Ord, not out, so the handsome young man in the passenger seat was not free for the weekend. She noticed his civilian clothes and long hair. The lady driving looked like his mother. He was probably about to start basic training, which meant eight weeks of going nowhere. And of course, Melanie lamented, the boy wasn't looking at her, he was looking at Nina. He stepped out of his car and cocked his head at the flat.

"Problems?" he asked, skillfully moving the jack. Then his head swung back to his own car. "This will only take a few minutes, Mom," he called. The lady didn't seem too pleased, but she nodded her head.

The boy looked a little too serious, Melanie decided, hardly the effervescent type that she preferred. Still, he was handsome, with his lantern jaw and sky-blue eyes and a muscular build.

"Thanks," Melanie said sweetly as the tire came off. Nina stood back, giving a sigh of boredom as her gaze drifted away. "Are you going into basic training?" Melanie asked.

He nodded and continued to concentrate on the tire.

"What's your name?"

"Cliff."

"Got a last name?" Melanie smiled.

"Cliff Weigel."

"Must be exciting, to be in the Army. You get to travel, meet people, see new things."

"Yeah."

"My friend and I live around here," Melanie volunteered. "In Castroville. That's not too far away."

The new tire went on with a clank and the lug bolts followed. Sweat dripped down the boy's face as he focused on his work, not responding to Melanie's cheerful chattering.

"You know what Castroville is famous for? Castroville is the Home of the Artichoke," Melanie continued, undaunted. "That's what the Castroville Chamber of Commerce says. We grow more artichokes than any other spot in the world. Brussels sprouts, too. It's a great place to live if you're a vegetarian . . ." Melanie knew she was babbling. When he finally did get his leave from the Army, Cliff would never want to date her. She wanted to tell him what a hopeless place Castroville was to live in, that he'd be trying to meet new people, too, if he was stuck there. Outside of school, there was little to do but see movies or drop coins in a video arcade. Every boy either wanted to be a farmer like his dad or run a filling station. As soon as she graduated from high school in June, Melanie was getting out. One of the world's tragedies, she would tell anyone who'd listen, was that she and her mother had been stranded in Castroville for three long years.

"Cliff," Melanie managed, taking a breath for courage, "do you mind if I ask you a personal question?"

"Shoot." He squinted up through the sun, his hair matted from the work.

You're so helpful and good-looking I want to pinch myself. I would like you to wrap your arms around me. Do you like me? Do you think you could learn to like me? Would you ever marry me and take me away from here?

"You were saying?" the boy asked.

"Nothing."

"What?"

"Oh nothing, it's all right," she said, suddenly feeling hopeless. "Really."

Melanie thanked Cliff and watched as he gave Nina another glance before he jumped back into his car and headed through the post entrance.

"What happened to you?" Nina said, shaking her head as Melanie drove them home. "You were supposed to give him your phone number, not the agriculture report on Castroville."

"What was the point? He's going to be tied up for eight weeks."

"There's always afterward."

"He was more interested in you," Melanie said.

"I've got a boyfriend. We weren't here for me."

"He wasn't my type anyway."

"Excuses," said Nina. "Whatever happened to Melanie the Fearless?"

Suddenly Melanie felt teary. "Maybe I lost my nerve."

"*You* lost your nerve? This whole crazy scheme was *your* idea—"

"Look, it could have happened to anyone."

"You're too much," Nina said, dropping her head back on the seat in exasperation. "Paul Newman could walk into your life and you wouldn't know what to do with him."

"Yes I would."

"Sure—and Superman takes a bath with a rubber duck."

2

The wind suddenly gusted, breaking the monotony of the hot, still afternoon and bringing temporary relief to the forty trainees of Charlie Company's Third Platoon. On the flat dirt expanse known as the Fort Ord parade grounds, dust devils sprang up and danced around them. The dirt coated the boys' exhausted faces and brought on raspy coughs. Cliff Weigel, one of the platoon's four squad leaders, peered ahead stoically. The day had included a three-mile run, two hours of marching formation, low crawling, and bayonet drill, but as Cliff studied his drill instructor he knew the punishment was hardly over. Staff Sergeant Clarence Bradshaw, attached to Charlie Company of the Second Battalion, Third Brigade, Seventh Infantry Division, paced in front of the scraggly formation, chin down, brooding—the lull before the storm. Without warning he pounced on a boy whose terror showed too quickly in his eyes.

"Front and center, Maggot Gibbons!" The sergeant's Smokey the Bear hat angled across B. J. Gibbons' pale face like a dark curtain. Another gust of wind filled the silence, punctuated by the crackle of M-16 fire from one of the beachfront rifle ranges. As Bradshaw glowered at B.J., Cliff wondered again what he thought of the young, baby-faced DI, his short hair as fuzzy as a teddy bear's. While he looked innocent, he was a certified fire-breather, cut from the same cloth as a dozen movie villains. Barracks wisdom said that Bradshaw's goal in life was to make everyone miserable, which made him easy to hate, but Cliff reserved judgment. The man had a tough job.

"Private Gibbons, what's 'CO' mean?" Bradshaw demanded. The other trainees stirred nervously, waiting out the ritual.

"It means 'commanding officer,' Sergeant," B.J. answered easily.

"Who's your company CO?"

"Captain Wentworth, Sergeant."

"Battalion?"

B.J. looked troubled. "Sergeant, that would be Major Stark."

"Brigade?"

Hesitation. "Colonel Donelson?"

"Lucky guess, boy. Now give me the chain of command—"

Cliff could see the panic setting in. He began to feel sorry for B.J. Only the second week of basic and the lanky, affable B.J. had already found himself Bradshaw's scapegoat. He got blamed for everything. Part of it was B.J.'s problem. He'd come into the platoon relaxed and carefree, as if basic training would hardly be more taxing than the ROTC course he said he'd taken in high school. Other boys had been sluggish or lazy, too, but overnight they'd transformed themselves for fear of Bradshaw. Mysteriously, B.J. held to his old ways.

"The chain of command, boy—" Bradshaw prodded.

Deep breath. Eyes trying to focus. "Sergeant, that would be a general, who has four stars, major general, with three stars, lieutenant general, with two stars—"

Cliff winced for B.J. Bradshaw extended his boot and stamped on the trainee's foot. "That's lieutenant general who has three stars, boy, *then* major general."

"Yes, Sergeant," B.J. echoed, humiliated, and continued the recitation. Concentration and composure lost, he stumbled twice more before Bradshaw finished with him, then sunk back crimson-faced into the platoon, looking for anonymity. Titters of laughter rippled through the ranks.

"All right, scumbuckets," Bradshaw interrupted, picking up two pugil sticks, "time to bash each other's head in."

Groans of objection filled the air as the drill instructor made a ten-foot-diameter circle in the dirt with his boot. The trainees formed themselves into a larger circle that ringed the arena of combat. "I need two volunteers," Bradshaw barked. "Two *men*." A whistle lanyard whipped around his finger as he paraded behind trainees, breathing on necks. "I don't want pussies, I want men, because today we're not

fighting with safety helmets on like we're sissy football players . . ."

Cliff stepped forward into the combat circle. There
were no raised eyebrows; everyone was used to seeing
him volunteer. He was on his way to becoming an
officer, he thought, so he had to react when leadership
was called for. Unlike B.J. and a lot of boys, Cliff
wasn't afraid of anything that Bradshaw or the Army
threw at him. He was in peak physical condition. He
was sure he could endure the regimen of basic training. He could shoot an M-16 more accurately, run a
faster mile, and reel off more push-ups than anyone in
his company of two hundred boys. The chain of command he could recite in his sleep. Most of the others
wondered about him, he knew, because he wasn't a
showboat like some trainees with lesser talents. He
usually kept to himself, even when there was time for
barracks socializing. He guessed he'd always been a
little out of step with his peers. In high school, instead
of hitting the beer party circuit, he'd been a loner
who'd done well at football, fixed up old cars, and
read military histories. He'd chosen the Army over
college, which set him apart even further from the
girls and guys who'd given up on getting to know
him.

"My, what chicken-livered maggots we have," the
sergeant observed as he scrutinized the tight, unflinching faces. "Someone's letting me down. You're
all letting me down. Are you maggots afraid of Private
Weigel?"

Someone would have to respond, thought Cliff. He
expected one of the more confident boys to join him,

but after a slight movement in the formation, eyes turning, it was B.J. who stepped into the circle.

"As I live and breathe," Bradshaw declared. A smile floated on his face, as if he couldn't wait for the platoon scapegoat to get clobbered.

Both boys picked up their weapons, long sticks with padding on each end the shape and size of a boxing glove, and faced each other coolly. Combat rules were simple. The winner was the one who knocked the other out of the circle with any blow above the belt.

Bradshaw's whistle shrilled in Cliff's ears. Maybe B.J. was trying to redeem himself. Cliff couldn't blame him because nothing was worse than being singled out for torture every day. B.J.'s face was a mix of resolve and desperation as he raised his stick and aimed for Cliff's ribs. When the blow was blocked, B.J. swung defiantly at his adversary's chest. Cliff was stung but there was no real damage. He was reluctant to strike back, at least hard. He knew B.J. was outmatched. One good strike from Cliff would send him reeling—but what was the point of that? Yet Cliff knew he couldn't stand around and risk angering Bradshaw.

Cliff didn't even understand the reason for the pugil sticks. It was hardly a skill one would use in combat. Maybe the sergeant just liked a little blood and gore. For a moment Cliff glimpsed the whitecaps of the Pacific in the distance, and closer in the highway that paralleled the fort, with cars coming and going. Everything seemed so peaceful. Unfocused, he was

19

caught by B.J.'s stick in the stomach and lost his breath.

Raucous cheering.

Embarrassed, Cliff circled B.J. in the tight arena and waited for an opening. With the quickness of a lizard's tongue, his stick darted toward B.J.'s neck and sent him sprawling. Cliff expected surrender, but B.J. picked himself gamely up and came at him again. Cliff deflected an uncertain swing and promptly clobbered B.J. in the face. He was sorry instantly as the blood spurted from the boy's nose. An eye fluttered closed.

"Go on, Weigel . . . finish him off . . . he's still standing!" Bradshaw roared.

Cliff hesitated. Bradshaw yelled again, echoed by a chorus of chanting trainees. Cliff's follow-up blow flashed into B.J.'s ribs. His face squinched in pain as he tumbled out of the circle and down on his butt.

Wild, wild cheering. B.J. looked like he'd been hit by a Mack truck. He tried to raise himself but a supporting arm gave way like a wobbly piling.

"This maggot needs a new pair of eyes," Bradshaw announced in disgust. He hovered over the supine body. "Private Gibbons, my grandmother's got better reflexes than you!"

When B.J. didn't stir, the sergeant sliced his boot into the rib cage he was tenderly protecting. B.J. rose lifelessly off the dirt. "Maggot, are you dead? Maggot, should I care?"

"Maybe he's hurt," someone offered.

"He will be now," Bradshaw answered, still furious, and delivered another boot to B.J.'s kidney. B.J. screamed but no sound came out. "Help this worm to the infirmary," Bradshaw barked to Cliff, who stood nearby. "I don't want to see his chicken-livered face in my platoon as long as I live."

"Want some help?" Cliff asked, offering his hand as B.J. edged slowly down the infirmary steps. His ribs had been heavily taped and he breathed with difficulty. Cliff thought of apologizing for the pugil stick blow, but B.J. had to have known the risks when he entered the circle.

"I'll be all right," he managed. The voice was proud and independent, yet B.J. looked totally frustrated as they marched back to the barracks and Bradshaw's private kingdom under the darkening sky. "The sergeant's really something, isn't he?" he said suddenly. "I got into the pugil circle with you when no one else would, and Bradshaw doesn't say a word about my courage . . . You know what the medic asked me? He wanted to know how I got so beat up. I said I took a fall on the afternoon run."

B.J.'s tone was intimate, as if he wanted Cliff to understand what he was enduring, wanted a friend or an ally. B.J. wasn't unliked by the others in the barracks, Cliff knew, he mixed well with his affable, breezy style, yet it was Cliff's approval he wanted now. B.J. was a bright kid, too, and good-looking. Like Cliff, he was supposed to attend Officer Candidate School after finishing basic training and another eight weeks of advanced individual training, but at the moment he seemed lost. Maybe he thought that after basic things would be easier. That was naive, Cliff knew. Unless B.J. changed, there would always be more Bradshaws to confound him.

"Bradshaw's not so bad," Cliff ventured. "He's just got a job to do."

"Last week he didn't care when someone got stuck with a bayonet, or that kid in the third squad broke his arm on the obstacle course. And not letting us wear helmets with the pugil sticks today . . . Is that his job? He's crazy."

"Give him a chance," Cliff argued.

"I don't think the guy's got both oars in the water, that's all."

Cliff didn't reply. B.J. looked disappointed but seemed resigned to the silence, as if he should have known that Cliff was too gung-ho Army ever to criticize Sergeant Bradshaw. As the two boys approached the company street, forty lobster-faced trainees of the Second Platoon thundered past them in a running formation, gasping for breath as they headed for their own barracks. In front of the mess hall a line was starting to form. Trainees stood silently at parade rest as they waited for permission to enter. Cliff motioned for B.J. to join him for dinner, but he shook his head and drifted away.

In the empty barracks B.J. unlaced his combat boots, pained by his sore ribs, and dropped onto his bunk. The place smelled of shoe polish, and Brasso, a reminder of work still to be done before morning formation. Right now he was too exhausted to do anything. He was hungry, too, but after the humiliation in the pugil circle he didn't want to face anyone. Better to get a little rest, he figured. Half-dozing, he thought about Cliff. Basically B.J. liked him. He realized he even admired him for his obvious strengths.

22

Maybe there was a little envy, too. Cliff was cool, calm, and collected, the perfect soldier. B.J. wondered why he couldn't excel like that.

But he knew, really. He didn't have the confidence. He had pretended everything in the Army would be easy because he wanted it to be easy; if it were too tough, he was afraid he couldn't handle it. His problems had started a long time before basic training. As a senior at John Quincy Adams High in Pittsburgh, Bernard Joseph Gibbons had been voted by his class as the boy most likely to succeed. People had looked up to him and respected him, B.J. knew, and why not? He dressed well, spoke entertainingly, got along with everyone, and did all right academically. As a junior he'd been class president, and last year vice-president of the student body. And girls, he couldn't forget about girls. He had always been popular, and could have settled down with any of a half dozen girl friends if he hadn't been heading for Boston College.

He thought college would be even better than high school. But that had been when his world began to cave in. He found that no matter how often he studied he didn't do well on tests or essays. The bull he'd thrown around so easily in high school wasn't enough to make good grades in college. Sure, he'd gotten into the school, but no one was impressed with him. He had doubts socially, too. Among the hordes of college students in Boston and Cambridge he felt anonymous and insecure. Maybe, he realized suddenly, he'd never had real self-confidence. Maybe the high school politics and extracurricular activities were covering up for his self-doubt. He'd just been trying to prove things to himself. B.J. knew he was in trouble even

23

before professors and his freshman advisor began telling him so. By Christmas vacation he was forced to drop out, which was when his real terror began. How did the boy most likely to succeed explain to everyone back home so early and obvious a failure?

He felt certain his parents wouldn't understand, and neither would old friends. Bobby Douglas, in the class below B.J.'s, had modeled his high school political career after B.J.'s, and the two had played on the basketball team. Bobby half-seriously expected B.J. to run for governor of Pennsylvania one day, and B.J., not minding the flattery, had never discouraged the idea. When Bobby learned about his dropping out, B.J. had lied that college wasn't the challenge he was looking for. When he saw his friend's face showed disappointment, he knew he never could admit the truth. After Christmas B.J. applied to several advertising and public relations firms, but the economy was still floundering, and the few openings were reserved for college grads. He actually considered working in a steel mill, but his ego was too big to allow him to call himself blue-collar. The boy most likely to succeed had to do something. Within a few weeks he visited the Army recruiting office. The Army had plenty of openings, the sergeant told him, and there would be another chance for college at Uncle Sam's expense, once B.J. became an officer. Everyone back home was pleased again, B.J. included. Maybe one day he'd make general, they said. He had pushed all his self-doubt down to where he didn't have to deal with it and smiled as he thought of his future in the Army.

When B.J. woke he didn't know how long he'd been sleeping. The dark barracks resounded with soft snoring and the occasional squeak of bed springs. Through a cracked window he studied the cusp of the moon angling toward a gray ocean. Nights were his favorite time. No one to hassle him, no pressures—and the illusion of privacy. He tried to forget his hunger and his dismal day as he retrieved a flashlight from his footlocker and dropped back on his bed with the letter he'd received that morning. From the return address he knew it was Bobby again. His friend wrote more often than B.J.'s parents.

Greetings, Supreme Allied Commander!

So how is Uncle Sam treating you these days? From your last letter it sounds like you're sailing through with flying colors, which doesn't surprise me. College was just an aberration for you. Maybe they'll make you a second lieutenant right after basic training! School continues to be a drag. It's really not the same since you left, B.J. When you were the student body vice-president there was a lot of school spirit; now it's nothing but individual egos. No leadership, I guess. Take our basketball team. We've lost nine straight and no one cares. If you were still here, I think we'd be winning. You know, sometimes I'm glad I lost the student body president election, because it would definitely be un-in-spir-ing to lead these *goofuses. I forgot to tell you . . . Sheri, your old girlfriend? She broke her leg trying a double flip at halftime, but she refuses to give up her cheerleader sweater even though her leg's in a cast for three months. I guess she's insecure. You remember Mr. Crandall, the auto shop teacher? Last week the guy won the state lottery—$3 million—and the next day he told the principal to stuff the auto shop in his ear. Old Crandall was really bitter. It makes you wonder, doesn't it? And how about Stevie Hower— or maybe your folks didn't tell you. It was in all the papers. Stevie was always a little wacko, but on Senior Day he outdid himself. Climbed the flag pole, took off all his clothes, and sat there until the police came. He never said why. Very funny. I mean, why can't anyone be serious anymore? I tell you, B.J., I can't wait to get out of this asylum.*

Write soon, okay?
Bobby

B.J. read the letter twice before clicking off his flashlight and staring into the darkness. The lies he'd written Bobby about being a success in basic suddenly embarrassed him. He felt homesick, too. Bobby Douglas, not Stevie, was the crazy one. Bobby didn't know how good he had it in high school. B.J. would give anything to jump into a time machine and travel back a year or two. To be looked up to again instead of being the platoon whipping boy . . .

A noise rose from under the barracks floorboards and broke his concentration. B.J. had listened to it before, almost whenever he woke during the night—a quick skittering of tiny feet. An intimate little party was going on between the floor joists. Two mornings ago he'd spotted one of the furry little monsters, wet and black, as it scurried across the latrine. The United States Army had rats.

He tried to sleep but his mind wouldn't click off. High school. It was all so easy to imagine he was still there. Hey, come off it, he thought suddenly, angry with himself. The past was behind him. It was time to grow up. Somehow he was not only going to survive basic, he would be the best trainee that Sergeant Bradshaw ever saw. If he was a leader in high school, he could be a leader in the Army—just like Cliff. The resolve flooded over B.J. like a vision.

He turned the flashlight back on and pulled out some writing paper and

Dear Bobby,

Got your letter today. It was fun to hear all the gossip. Tomorrow starts the third week of basic. Things have been a little rougher than I've let on, actually, but I think I've turned the corner. Right now I feel confident about the future. The Army might not make me a second lieutenant right after basic, but sooner or later those brass bars are going to be gleaming on my shoulders . . .

3

Nina had spent thirty minutes in front of her makeup mirror. She had been lucky with her looks, she often thought—blonde hair that fell to her shoulders, skin that obligingly tanned but never burned, a swimsuit figure to complement her long legs. Beauty *and* brains, the recently published senior yearbook said. As she sat back now on the living-room couch, conscious that her shoulders were drooping, she took a relaxing breath. The reporter from the Castroville *Times*, a severe-looking woman who kept brushing her hair from her eyes, paused to study the modest McKenzie living room, then continued the interview.

Q: Nina, you were captain of your debate team last year?

A: Yes. This year, too.

Q: And you're on the swim team, a member of the honor society, and you were elected vice-president of the senior class?

A: (blushing) That's right.

Q: You're a remarkable young woman. What or whom do you owe your success to?

A: I guess my mother and father. They've always been supportive. They encourage me to work hard, and they taught me that I could accomplish whatever I set my mind to.

Q: So you credit others with your success.

A: I didn't exactly say that. I do things myself.

Q: You mentioned that in September you're enrolling at the University of California at Davis. Didn't you also tell me you were accepted at Berkeley and Stanford—better schools academically. Why Davis?

A: My boyfriend will be going to Davis. You probably know Billy Johnson's family. They own the largest farm in the area. Billy's going to major in agriculture, and Davis is the top agriculture school in the West.

Q: But you're not going to major in agriculture—

A: I really don't know.

Q: That's a little hard to believe, isn't it? Nina, you're a girl who's accomplished so much—surely you have a mind of your own that's been concentrating on your future.

A: (forcing a smile) I think a person can have her own mind and still be undecided about some things.

Q: That's nicely put. I'd like to quote you exactly. There's one last thing our readers usually like to know on profile pieces. Life seems so easy for you, Nina—a breeze. Do you feel as if you have a lucky star over your shoulder?

A: I've been very fortunate that way. Things have always fallen into place for me.

It was after five when the reporter snapped a final photo of Nina for the profile of the "Castroville High Outstanding Senior." The article would appear next weekend, but Nina didn't feel as good about it as she wanted. She resented the reporter's little dig about not having a mind of her own. The piece would also make her sound like a goody two shoes, as if she didn't have a wild side. Maybe she hadn't shown much of one so far, but she liked to think it was still there.

Her parents, of course, would be proud of the interview. It was the Nina they had shaped and molded for seventeen years. Three decades before Nina, Frank and Emily McKenzie had graduated from Castroville High—"eternal sweethearts" declared the senior yearbook that Nina had once glimpsed—and were married two years later. When her father fractured his hip and spent a year convalescing, Nina's mother was forced to leave college to work. Neither one had found the time or money to go back for a degree. Life hadn't been easy for them, Nina knew. Eventually her mother became a legal secretary and her father was promoted to department store manager in nearby Monterey. Both wanted for Nina the opportunities they never had for themselves. They had lavished on their only daughter the love, time, and energy to nurture a future corporate president. Great things were expected of Nina, and so far everything had fallen into place. Her parents hoped Nina would marry Billy, after the two graduated from college, and settle on the farm Billy would take over from his father, and that then Nina could raise children while teaching evenings at Monterey Peninsula College. Later, when the children had flown the nest, she might teach full time or tackle another career altogether.

Everything was all figured.

Or was it? Sometimes Nina wondered about the future. When she was growing up, college had seemed distant and abstract, nothing to worry about, but lately she'd been uneasy. Was college and a future in Castroville what she *really* wanted? Had she changed, or was she still changing, from the person who had done all the planning? The fact that things were so easy and convenient added to her anxiety. What if there came a time when things *didn't* go smoothly and she wouldn't know what to do? Somehow she didn't feel prepared. She didn't feel she knew what the real world was like.

It was Melanie who'd helped plant that idea in her head. "You're just playing it safe," Melanie would say. "You're never going to know how to live, not if you stay in Castroville. You think your life's a success—all your friends may tell you that—but it isn't really. You're just hiding from life." When Nina demanded to know what that meant, Melanie gave her both barrels. "It's pretty clear, isn't it? You've never lived your own life. You've lived the life your parents wanted you to live. You're not in touch with your own feelings." Nina was stunned for a moment, then she bristled. "Melanie, who do you think you are—Sigmund Freud? You don't know what you're talking about. It's all clichés. You're just babbling as usual," she added with her characteristic sarcasm. It was how she talked when she felt insecure.

But Melanie the Philosopher had brought up the

subject more than once, and it had begun to seep in with Nina. What were her true feelings anyway?

Nina peeked out the kitchen window when she heard a car in the driveway. Her mother and father sat talking in the front seat, laughing about something, yet they looked tired as usual. Beyond, Nina's gaze lifted to the row of small stucco houses that dotted her street, their front lawns still brown from the cold winter. The road was scarred with potholes. The first artichoke fields were visible where the town proper ended and prosperity began. Even with the sky streaked with red, the immediate townscape looked bleak and depressing to Nina. She quickly boiled water for the spaghetti, anticipating the dinner conversation. They'd all talk about Nina's interview with the local reporter; then the discussion would swing to her mother's or father's day—long hours, difficult supervisors, headaches that would spill over till tomorrow. It was as if her parents didn't fully enjoy their lives, Nina sometimes thought, as if they worked hard mostly to make life enjoyable for her. That always made her feel guilty, and she couldn't help wondering—even if she married Billy and lived comfortably—if she wouldn't spend the rest of her life sacrificing for *her* children. It was a vicious circle. What was the point of living if you didn't do something for yourself? Nina was reluctant to ask out loud.

She was setting the table when the phone shrilled.

"Greetings from another planet," the voice piped.

"I'll have to call you back, Melanie," said Nina. "Mom and Dad just drove up."

"This'll only take a second," Melanie insisted. "Can you sign my petition tomorrow?"

"Which one?"

"The school dress code—"

"For the two punkers?" Melanie was forever circulating petitions around school, making her a sharp thorn in the side of the administration. She wasn't a punker herself, but Melanie insisted that kids should, within reason, dress any way they wanted. Nina pretty much agreed, but her parents winced every time she signed one of Melanie's petitions. "Okay, count me in," Nina said, then added mischievously, "but I expect you to get that Fort Ord trainee to sign, too—the one you let get away. What was his name anyway?"

Melanie said nothing, as if still embarrassed for her failure of nerve, and she was off on another tangent. Friday night there was going to be a fabulous concert in Monterey, and Melanie was about to drive over to the record store for tickets—

"I can't go," Nina stopped her.

"Why not?"

"Billy and I are steady for Friday. You know that."

Melanie groaned into the receiver.

"Don't blame me," Nina said. "What am I supposed to do?"

"Break your date," Melanie declared cheerfully. "Call Billy and say you've changed your mind."

"Very funny. I've never broken a date with Billy in my life. I don't even know if I want to."

"That's because you're chicken. You know what they say—'no guts, no glory.'"

"For someone who chickened out in front of a guy at Fort Ord, I don't think you should be preaching."

"That's different. We both know you're not really in love with Billy Johnson anyway. Sooner or later you're going to break up. Why not start now?"

Nina hung up in disgust.

After dinner she helped with the dishes and slipped off to her room to study. Trying to concentrate was futile. Her eyes swam to the vase with one long-stemmed American Beauty red rose that Billy had left for her—for no reason, he said, except that he was in love. Billy was almost perfect, even-tempered, conscientious, hard-working. A true-blue Boy Scout from a wealthy family, he was crazy about Nina. And she was crazy about him, or she acted as if she was. Hadn't they been going steady for over two years, and their parents been friends long before that? Didn't she and Billy have the same interests, go to the same church, enjoy the same friends? As her mother always asked, what could be better? But something didn't feel right. Even before Melanie got on her soapbox about Nina's life, Nina had felt sometimes that she was pretending with Billy. She was going with him because it was so easy; it was what everyone expected and wanted. She wondered if she even knew what being in love meant. It had to be more than what she felt for Billy.

I'll call him, Nina suddenly thought, looking at the phone. I'm not the chicken Melanie says I am. The only problem was what to say. Should she make up an excuse?—to say she was going to a concert with Melanie was pouring salt on the wound. Billy considered Melanie an oddball for carrying her petitions around, taking on the whole world. He couldn't understand what Nina saw in Melanie. It was so obvious to Nina—Melanie had a spirit of spontaneity and adventure, when everyone else in Castroville was plodding and predictable.

Nina dialed Billy's number. Part of her hoped he'd be out, but he answered cheerfully.

"Hi," she said after a beat.

"Don't tell me, you just got lonely . . . you had to talk to me." Billy had a reassuring voice, warm, almost melodious.

"Were we supposed to go out this Friday?" she asked casually.

"Is this amnesia? Of course. A movie and something to eat, or the other way around. Is something wrong?"

"Sort of," Nina said.

Silence.

"A girlfriend is coming to visit. I met her in Los Angeles last summer. Remember I told you about her? She's only here for the weekend, and she wanted to get together. I mean, how could I say no?"

"Let's make it a threesome at the movies. My treat. I don't mind."

"It's better if I see her alone. How else can we talk about you, Billy?" She laughed, but it sounded phony.

"Is this all on the level?" he asked suddenly. "I don't remember any LA friend."

"You know I'd rather be out with you, but Patty isn't that social—"

"Hey, this isn't some other guy? You've never broken a date with me . . ." He was uneasy, and sounded a little hurt.

Nina hated that this was turning out to be so hard. "How could you say that—some other guy? I told you, this is a girlfriend. I've never broken a date and I never will."

Billy was quiet. "Okay," he finally said, but he didn't hide the disappointment in his voice.

"You aren't mad at me, are you?" asked Nina. "I love you. I'll call you in the morning," Nina promised. He was suspicious, she thought. Maybe he had reason to be. But of what? There was no other guy. There was just an empty feeling.

Nina finished her homework and said goodnight to her parents. Sleep was impossible. You're an idiot, she told herself. You deserve to be shot for messing with your life. Why risk upsetting Billy and blowing the relationship? All this for a crummy concert—or to prove to Melanie that she could be independent. Or was she really trying to prove it to herself? What was the point?

She was wrong. She had to call Billy back.

But Nina didn't pick up the phone, and even in the morning, when she'd promised to call him, she only grabbed a quick breakfast and hurried off to school.

4

He was six years old again, and he saw himself clearly. He remembered the game. His mother had just moved the family to the San Fernando Valley, into an old stucco house with a tool shed in back that smelled of earth and insect spray. Cliff would stand quietly in front of the shed door and concentrate—pray, really—and very slowly, almost afraid to breathe, he would open the door. "You're back!" he shouted happily. Even before he'd run up to hug the gentle, handsome man inside he would hurry to tell his mother the news. "He's back! He came home!" "There's no one there, sweetie," she would reply, slipping a comforting arm around Cliff. "There's no one there at all," and she'd walk him back to the shed and they'd glance into the empty space.

The rough hands of the company clerk woke Cliff from his dream a few minutes before reveille. He slipped uneasily out of the coils of sleep and peered into the morning darkness. The clerk whispered that

Bradshaw wanted to see him on the QT. "What for?" he asked, but the Specialist Four only shrugged. In fresh fatigues, Cliff was out of the barracks before anyone stirred. Maybe there was an emergency back home, he thought as he passed the mess hall. What else could be so urgent at this hour? For all his desire to be disciplined, Cliff felt his stomach flutter.

He knocked on the company headquarters door, entering with a smart salute to the CO, a captain who left the day-to-day business of toughening up the trainees to a cadre of lieutenants and drill instructors. Even the lieutenants had little contact with trainees; the job of disciplining was entrusted to the platoon DI's, like Bradshaw.

Cliff found his sergeant behind a battered metal desk, moodily digging a spoon into a grapefruit, the sullen face unhappy about something. Bradshaw looked up and said nothing. As Cliff waited, he realized how little he knew about his drill instructor. According to one of the cooks, Bradshaw might look only eighteen but he was twenty-five. From the South, the son of a Fundamentalist preacher, he had a rigid sense of right and wrong. He had never been to college. He'd made the Army his career, and he was a physical fitness addict. Cliff thought they had a lot in common.

"You wanted to see me, Sergeant?" he spoke clearly. The jarring sound of reveille broke over the loudspeakers outside.

"At ease." Bradshaw tossed the grapefruit rind into a wastebasket and lounged back in his swivel chair. His hands stretched behind his head. "How come you're so tense, Weigel?"

38

"I was wondering why you wanted to see me, Sergeant. Is my family okay?"

"Your family's fine so far as I know," Bradshaw answered. "But your Army buddies are in major trouble."

Cliff didn't understand.

"Private, do you know what 'BA' stands for?"

"No, Sergeant."

"Take a guess."

Cliff shrugged. "I really don't know."

Bradshaw squinted back. "It stands for bad attitude. BAD ATTITUDE!"

For a moment Cliff thought Bradshaw was talking about him, but that was impossible. He knew he was the top trainee in his platoon if not the whole company. He was proud of it, too.

"Some people around here say that the Third Platoon's got nothing but *BA* trainees. They say we're the sorriest mothers who ever marched the face of the earth. The other drill sergeants—my *friends*—think we're hopeless. What do you think, Weigel?"

"Maybe they're right," Cliff offered, guessing that was what Bradshaw wanted to hear.

"BA Dingbats, that's what they're calling us. *Dingbats!*"

"Yes, Sergeant."

"Well they're WRONG!"

Cliff held his breath.

"We're tough, Weigel. We're not afraid of anything."

"Yes, Sergeant."

"I'm going to prove it, too." Bradshaw levered himself forward, as if to confide a secret. "I made my drill

39

sergeant pals a little bet last night." His eyes flicked up to Cliff. "And you're going to help me win it."

The suggestion of enlisting Cliff's aid made him feel a bond with his sergeant overcoming his bad feeling from Bradshaw's voice. Still, he didn't know what to make of this. Was there supposed to be betting in basic training?

"Private Weigel, have you ever wakened in the middle of the night in your barracks?"

He shook his head. He was a sound sleeper.

"Stay up later tonight. That's an order. You're going to hear something under the floorboards."

What? he wondered. Ghosts?

The sergeant threw him a wink. "Rats, boy. You're going to hear lots of rats."

The expression on Bradshaw's face startled Cliff. There was almost a glow of anticipation. He was planning something that would bring him pleasure. Cliff felt uneasy. And where did the bet come in?

"Saturday night the five platoons of Charlie Company are going hunting," Bradshaw continued, folding his hands on the desk. "We're going to have ourselves a little contest."

"What kind of contest?" Cliff asked innocently.

The sergeant grinned. "We're going to see which platoon can catch the most rats."

Cliff pretended to understand.

"I'm putting you in charge, Weigel. You're my best man. You organize the other squad leaders. Just make sure of one thing—"

Arching his brow, Cliff waited.

"We damn sure better win."

"Yes, Sergeant." Cliff turned and departed, puzzling over the visit with Bradshaw. Was the sergeant serious about a rat hunt? How did it prove manhood or bravery? It sounded sick. And to call him out of bed to tell him . . . Cliff thought about what B.J. had said en route from the infirmary. Maybe he was right. Maybe the good sergeant didn't have both his oars in the water after all.

5

Melanie guided her Chevy convertible up to the curb of Burt's Burger Bowl and beeped the horn twice. As she waited for her mother to finish work, she stared up Castroville's main street, past gas stations and small groceries and nondescript brick office buildings. The town seemed deserted, like a string of lonely bus stops. How anyone could spend an entire lifetime in Artichoke City was incomprehensible to Melanie. She avoided downtown whenever possible, but with only one car in the family she had to pick her mother up at Burt's.

A few blocks away the two-story high school peeked above the flat streetscape, frail and ready to collapse from age. A call to arms, CASTROVILLE TIGERS was emblazoned across the top of the building. Melanie usually escaped with the three o'clock bell. She didn't feel close to anyone but Nina. Sometimes, if Nina had free time, they would study together, but her friend was usually at an honors society meeting or working out with the swim team or something. Everyone loved Nina, Melanie knew, but it was the kind of adoration that had strings attached. We love you because you're good for the school and the community. Be like me, Melanie thought, and they wouldn't love you so much.

"Hi, honey," Doris Connors interrupted her thoughts. The fake corsage on her waitress uniform looked wilted enough to be real. Doris, weary, sat herself on the hot vinyl seat and mussed her hair into place. She was attractive in many ways, Melanie judged, with her thick red hair and a lean, sculpted face that Melanie liked to remember as sparkling but now usually looked passive. After the divorce and the move to Castroville, her mother had lost something. She didn't date or travel, she didn't even like to take in a movie. She chose to lead a lonely life, and Melanie often thought that if she ever let her guard down the same fate could happen to her. The idea depressed and scared her. The two summers her mother had made Melanie work at Burt's were more miserable than any nightmare—boring work, boring people—and no one realized what a dead end it was but Melanie. The only redeeming feature of the summers was that she'd saved escape money—and the knowledge that she wouldn't have to go back again. After graduation, her mother agreed, Melanie was free to do as she wanted.

"Hey, I've got a great idea," Melanie declared. The car engine turned over with a troubling whine. "Let's drive over to Carmel. That shopping mall just opened—"

"I think we should get home, baby," Doris said. "Somebody has to cook dinner."

Melanie heard the self-pity but ignored it. "Come on, we can eat out. It won't be that expensive. Then we can go shopping."

"Maybe this weekend."

Melanie knew it would never happen. They'd end up on the moon before they bought something in pricey Carmel. Melanie used to argue with her mother but now they lived a peaceful if delicate coexistence. Melanie steered the car through the flat stretches of artichoke fields, listening to her mother complain that she'd never sat down once all day. Melanie wasn't proud that her mother was a waitress—she wanted something better for her—but outside of working in the fields there weren't many job opportunities in Castroville, so Doris was lucky to have a full-time work, even if it gave her sore legs. They had moved here from northern Oregon on the promise of an agricultural administrative position, only to learn upon arrival that the federal government had abandoned that project. Melanie voted to move back to Oregon, but Doris had too many bad memories from the divorce. Nothing as appealing as an office job came open. Eventually a welcome mat was found at Burt's Burger Bowl. With tips Doris brought home enough money to rent a small house that once was a farm cottage, provide three meals, and support a clunker of a car. Luxuries they could forget about.

After dinner Melanie retreated to her room with her algebra book, but it was hard to get interested in the problems. Two ditch diggers were digging twice as fast as they had dug yesterday . . . women in a bridge club were lying about their ages . . . She closed the textbook and retrieved a large, flat envelope hidden in her closet. The eight-by-ten color glossy photo was nestled inside, just as she'd left it. The boy in the West Point uniform was named Steve Coughlin, and Melanie's camera had caught him on a Central Park bench, the afternoon light playing on his dignified face. He was a plebe, he had informed Melanie when they met in New York two summers ago. They had been introduced at Melanie's friend's in New York City, where she was staying for a week after her father, as a guilt-offering after the divorce, had bought her a round-trip ticket east. She had never been in so exciting a city as New York. And she was sure she'd fallen in love with the boy from West Point. She knew she was being impulsive, but the combination of his uniform, looks, and kind personality were irresistible. They had gone dancing one night, to a movie another, and to a fine French restaurant the third. Then Steve had to return to the Academy. She'd been afraid to tell him how she felt about him because he might not take her seriously; after all, they just met. But returning home she couldn't forget him, and began to write often.

They corresponded for a few months before Steve revealed that he had a steady girlfriend back home in St. Louis. Then he stopped writing. Melanie tried to phone him at West Point but he never took the calls. Her letters went unanswered. She was crushed. Her mother tried to console her but she couldn't accept that Steve didn't want her. Who would ever want her? she wondered. The divorce was fresh in her mind. Her father had fought with her mother and walked out. How could he leave his daughter, too? He knew she loved him. He said he loved her, too, yet he didn't even ask her to come with him.

It had taken Melanie ages to get over Steve and her parents' splitting up. Maybe she'd never gotten over them. People just didn't come through for her, she'd begun to think. She'd dated other boys since Steve but nothing had developed into a relationship. The local boys were either too self-important, too demanding, or too cruel. After a few dates her novelty wore off and they'd find Melanie too independent or not pretty enough or something. She had begun to think the problem might be her. Maybe she wasn't lucky when it came to relationships. Maybe she never would be. Behind her facade of confidence she was a trembling sea of insecurity.

Melanie took a leisurely shower until the hot water gave out. In bed, she pulled a stack of magazines from a bedside table and splayed them in front of her. Stunning models, a skyline shot of Manhattan, an intimate restaurant with two lovers gazing into each other's eyes. This was living, she told herself. The beautiful clothes, good taste, the money to live well. This was what freedom was all about.

The photograph of the West Point cadet was still on her bed. She raised the picture to her lips and kissed it, as if the young man on it were somehow real. She would never tell anyone she did that, not even Nina. As she drifted to sleep, the picture stayed beside her, a companion in the darkness warding off the chill of loneliness.

6

Somebody was talking in his sleep. Cliff sat up and listened, watched. He dropped back on his pillow and tried to sleep. What was bothering him? His mind wouldn't turn off. He listened for the rats skittering between the floor joists as Bradshaw had ordered, but all he heard was someone stirring on his bunk.

He squinted through the darkness as the figure awakened and reached down to open his footlocker. He moved jerkily as he pulled out a pair of pants—civilian jeans. But that was impossible, Cliff thought. No one had civilian clothes. The boy slipped into the jeans and added a sweatshirt and a pair of sneakers. Cliff got up.

"Jesus!" the boy whispered in fright when Cliff touched his shoulder.

Cliff couldn't believe it. B.J. looked at him with alarm.

"What do you think you're doing?" Cliff asked.

B.J. took a resigned breath, as if it was pointless to lie about the obvious. "What's it look like?"

"You're going AWOL."

"Listen, I've got to get out. Maybe just for tonight, but I have to get out. I'm going nuts in the Army."

"You can't leave."

"Don't worry, I won't get caught."

"I can't let you go AWOL. I'm your squad leader, remember?" Cliff knew he sounded severe and righteous, but he meant it. He didn't make the rules, he just obeyed them.

"Hey, come off it, will you?" B.J. said. "I've been planning this for days. I sneaked over to the PX last night for these clothes and I've got about twenty bucks left for a night on the town." He spun away, moving toward the door, when Cliff confronted him again.

"You're making trouble for the whole platoon if Bradshaw finds out," Cliff warned. "He could punish everyone."

"I don't give—"

"You should."

B.J. stepped back, as if he didn't believe this was happening. He was failing at a midnight escape, just like he'd failed at everything else in the Army. Despite his resolve to do better. Bradshaw had continued to pick on him during the week, undermining his confidence. B.J. needed a breather, a perspective. Why couldn't Cliff see that?

"Tell me one thing, Weigel," he snapped, "how come you're so gung-ho Army? I can't even figure why you're in the Army. You're smart, you're capable, you could have done a lot of smart-boy things, like gone to college. So what are you doing here—and why do you act so damn perfect? I mean, haven't you wanted to get out of this place for a night?"

"No," Cliff answered honestly.

"Then I guess you're as crazy as Bradshaw," said B.J. "You and Sarge must be best of friends." B.J. lurched away, determined to get out. Cliff grabbed for him but stumbled in the darkness. When he looked up he saw the blur of B.J.'s fist. He crashed down, banging into another footlocker. Blood dripped from his nose and his head spun. "That's for the pugil circle," B.J. whispered defiantly, and darted out.

Cliff raised himself slowly. His nose was still bleeding. The other trainees had missed the nighttime drama, he saw as he maneuvered back to B.J.'s bunk. As the peaceful snores rose around him, Cliff stowed everything back inside B.J.'s locker in case the duty officer wandered through the barracks. For a moment he sympathized with B.J. Maybe a night on the town for B.J. was what the doctor ordered. Wouldn't Cliff go a little crazy if the sergeant treated him like he did B.J.? But Cliff definitely didn't see himself in the same category as their drill sergeant, and he couldn't help resenting B.J. for making the comparison. Didn't he think that Cliff was his own man? Cliff wondered how his father would have handled the situation. What was the line between being Army-by-the-book and being an individual?

As he finished straightening up B.J.'s area he spotted a couple of letters in one corner of the footlocker. Hesitating, Cliff pulled out B.J.'s flashlight and dropped to the floor.

Hey General,

Spring has finally sprung in old Pittsburgh, Pa. The grass is greening, and seniors are going out of their minds. In one week a certain band of merry pranksters put a smoke-bomb in Mrs. Steadfast's purse, streaked a girls' P.E. class, and locked poor Mr. Burley out of his own classroom. You remember how it was, B.J. What we have here is an asylum run by the inmates. Stevie Hower has really gone off the deep end now. After sitting naked on the flagpole last week, he's telling everyone he's going to become a missionary in New Guinea (True!) It's all kind of liberating, except if you're the one who's not sure what to do with his future. I got accepted at Rutgers, Pitt, and Ohio, and I'm on the waiting list at Brown. My problem is bucks. My parents can chip in, but even with a scholarship and a part-time job I don't know if I can afford college. Maybe a student loan would help. Maybe state college would be best. And I'm still thinking about the Army because then Uncle Sam could pay for my education. Give me an update, pal. Uh-oh, some friends just pulled up at the curb with water balloons in the back seat. One question for you, B.J: When you finally graduate from this madness, are you officially an adult?

See ya,
Bobby

Cliff let the flashlight dance over the words of an unfinished letter.

> *Dear Bobby,*
> *Really enjoyed your last letter. It's great to*
> *hear about the home front. I've got to admit, I*
> *miss it a lot. I keep thinking of that one basket-*
> *ball game last year, against Hamilton, when*
> *you passed me the ball and I made a layup*
> *with two seconds to go. What a victory, huh? I*
> *was so scared I'd blow it, scared what people*
> *would think if I did . . .*

Cliff felt embarrassed and tucked B.J.'s letter back in the footlocker. He had never read someone else's mail, but there was something intriguing about B.J. The kid was unsure of himself, and he tried to cover it up. Cliff had known a lot of kids like that, yet in the confines of the Army he felt he knew B.J. better than he had anyone in high school. Beneath B.J.'s insecurity and frustration was a well-meaning honesty, a desire to do the right thing, and Cliff admired that. The surprise fist to his head notwithstanding, he thought suddenly, he hoped that B.J. had a good time tonight.

Melanie pulled her Chevy up to Nina's at exactly twenty to nine. Her friend was waiting at the curb and jumped in. "What are you doing out here?" Melanie asked.

"I've been waiting for an hour. I kept thinking Billy might call and ask to speak to me and my friend. I didn't exactly tell Mom. She thinks you and I are going to a movie."

"Relax," Melanie said, as she shifted into second and cruised toward the highway. "You're going to love the concert."

"I feel rotten about lying to Billy."

"It was a white lie, and white lies don't count. Besides, I bet you meet someone really special tonight."

"What's that mean?"

"A new boy. Someone who'll make you forget Billy."

"You're incredible, Melanie. Maybe I don't want to forget Billy."

"Sure you do." Melanie beamed. "Why else would you be going out tonight with me?"

The park was jammed for the concert. Melanie ran interference, leading Nina over and around bodies comfortably stretched in the cool grass. Floodlights illuminated the scaffolding and stage. The crowd began to clap for the music to begin. Melanie made her way as close to the stage as possible and spread out a blanket, nudging away intruders. A couple of girls from Castroville sat nearby. So what, Melanie thought, when they only waved to Nina. In another month, after graduation, Melanie would never have to see them again.

As the concert began Melanie sat back, and she was beginning to relax to the beat when she noticed the boy next to her. His attention was only half on the music. Every minute he'd sneak a glance at Melanie. At first she felt flattered, then she began to study the boy more carefully. His clothes were baggy and didn't fit, and he had a crew cut. Army? she guessed, but she doubted he was an officer. He looked too young. Probably he was in basic training, but then how could he be at the concert? When the boy caught Melanie staring back, she ignored his gaze and shrugged as if uninterested.

"Hi," he said, adding a generous smile.

Melanie looked away. Here was a chance but she wasn't in the mood for being picked up.

"Ever seen this band before?" the boy asked, undaunted. His hand reached out. "My name's B.J."

Actually he was cute, she decided, noticing long, lanky arms and an angular face, but much too pushy. "If you don't mind, I'm trying to listen to the music," Melanie answered.

A shaken B.J. retracted his hand. Part of the problem, he knew, was he was nervous about being AWOL, especially after the send-off from Cliff. Running from the barracks and avoiding the main road, he had crawled under the barbed-wire fence by the PX, hitched into Monterey while looking over his shoulder, and once in town noticed a poster about the concert. But now he couldn't believe this girl was ignoring him. She was attractive, and slightly snobby—he sort of liked that. But why didn't she like him? No girl back home had treated him like this. What was left of B.J.'s battered ego crumbled a little more. Yet he knew he couldn't let the encounter end disastrously. His reason for going AWOL was to rejoin the ranks of the living, wasn't it?

"I love this song," B.J. continued to Melanie. "The beat's really clever. Do you like it? No, let me guess," he laughed, "you probably can't stand it. You look unhappy about something."

Melanie sighed. She glanced toward Nina but she was caught up in the music, and indifferent to Melanie's problem. "Just what do you want?" Melanie said to B.J. She wasn't sure what she wanted herself.

"Just tell me your name."

"Melanie Connors."

"Pretty name. It's kind of poetic. You live around here or go to school?"

"Castroville High. I'm a senior."

"Terrific," said B.J.

Melanie tossed her head back. "What's so terrific about it? Unless it means that I'm almost free."

"Right," B.J. agreed, but he was surprised by her tone. Didn't Melanie know how lucky she was to be in school?

"And what about you? You're in the Army, aren't you?"

B.J. nodded reluctantly, trying not to show his embarrassment. "Right now I'm in basic training, but I'm going to Officer Candidate School." He watched a soft, approving smile come to Melanie's lips. Maybe he'd said the magic words. "Do you know something about the Army?" he asked.

"A little." The smile was suddenly eclipsed by a searching frown. "I thought that in basic training you never got leave—"

"My sergeant gave me a special pass," B.J. improvised, "for being the top trainee in the platoon."

"That's great," Melanie said sincerely. "And you're really going to be an officer?"

54

"Sure am," he said, and suddenly he wanted it to be true. B.J. saw her eyes parade over him, maybe imagining him with brass bars on his shoulder.

"Why don't you join my friend and me for the rest of the concert?" Melanie said. "You look kind of lonely. Poor soldier boy," she added, teasing him gently.

"I don't want to intrude—"

"Come on." Melanie made room for B.J. on the blanket and introduced him to Nina. She thought he was impressed with Nina's looks—what boy wasn't—but Nina was so into herself tonight that she hardly came across as warm. B.J. turned his attention back to Melanie. After another song she complained of being cold and B.J. slipped his arm around her. The music buoyed her mood even more. She was floating. This was nice, this was a surprise, she thought, stretching back on the blanket. There was something natural and easy-going about B.J. that made her feel comfortable. It was hard to believe they'd just met.

"Can I ask you something?" She turned to B.J. "And don't think this is crazy, okay?"

"Shoot."

"What do you think of me?"

B.J. looked surprised by the question, not sure how to answer.

"I don't really know you."

"I'm different from a lot of girls," Melanie answered for him. "I speak my mind. Some people think I'm too strong. Can you deal with that?"

"I don't know," he said after a moment. "But I like people like you."

Melanie was relieved to hear it.

"Life's so short," she observed. "If you feel strongly about something, why keep it inside?"

B.J. suddenly thought about how much he'd wanted to confront Sergeant Bradshaw, but courage wasn't his strong suit. He couldn't help but admire Melanie if it was hers. The concert ended with a drum solo and an explosion of flashing lights. When quiet descended over the park and everyone milled toward the exits, B.J. remained on the blanket with Melanie. Nina stood awkwardly, as if wanting to leave.

"You know, if I didn't have music in my life," Melanie announced to B.J., "I don't think I could be happy. Could you?" B.J. could tell that she hoped he would agree with her.

"I mean," Melanie explained, "aren't there certain things in life that you can't live without? There are for me—music, a good friend or two, something to look forward to . . ."

"Sure," B.J. said automatically, but then he thought about Melanie's points. There was nothing *he* looked forward to, and maybe that was one of his problems. Lately his life had been a catalog of failures and disappointments. He needed something or someone to lift him out of his rut, give him hope. He could only think of Melanie.

"Hey, the night's just starting," he said. "Have you got a car?"

"Where do you want to go?"

"Nowhere," came a firm voice. Nina had her arms folded over her chest and focused coolly on Melanie. "We have to get home," she explained to B.J.

"No we don't," said Melanie.

"Yes we do."

"It's only a little past eleven."

"Melanie, I *have* to go." Nina's emphatic tone ended the discussion.

B.J. was disappointed but he rebounded quickly. "How about next weekend?" It was a dumb thing to say—it would be impossible—but the words popped out.

Melanie tossed her head back, and gave Nina a vengeful glance. "I'd love to. But can you get a date for my friend, too?"

*"What?"*said Nina.

"We love to double date, don't we?" Melanie said to Nina. She glanced back at B.J. "You can find someone for Nina, can't you?"

"Oh . . . sure . . . no problem . . . Where shall we meet you?" he said, smooth as cream. B.J. nodded as Melanie named a restaurant in Monterey. He gave Melanie's hand a parting squeeze. He'd really wanted to kiss her but didn't have the nerve. His euphoria lasted a long minute before B.J. realized what a fool he was. The lies had flown thick and fast. Who did he think he was? He'd been so anxious he'd promised Melanie the moon, and yet, joining the crowd as it spilled out of the park, he knew he had to find a way to come through. Seeing Melanie again seemed like the most heartening thing in his dismal life. All he had to do was find someone to join his next escape.

Walking back to Fort Ord along the highway, B.J. froze when two MPs rolled up in a jeep, paralleling him as each grabbed a second glance at the figure in civilian clothes. B.J. lowered his head and kept moving. A pit opened in his stomach as he waited for a tap on the shoulder. Hello stockade. Goodbye lieutenant's bars.

But with the cackle of their two-way radio, the MPs raced on. B.J. lifted his head and gazed back on the park as he thought about the night of freedom and Melanie. Sweet dreams, he laughed, and realized the best thing of all was that they were real.

7

"You're very funny," Nina called as she half-chased Melanie out of the park to their car. "What were you trying to prove tonight—getting me a blind date . . . It was bad enough we saw Annie and Debra. What if they tell Billy?"

"I just want you to have fun too," Melanie declared.

"Do tell."

"You're too serious most of the time. Ms. Practicality. Down deep there's another side struggling to get out. That's why you hang around me."

"Melanie the Psychologist. You know how I feel when I'm around you?" Nina said. "I feel like we're the Odd Couple."

"I take that as a compliment." Melanie guided the old convertible onto the highway, letting the breeze muss her hair.

"Your problem is you're not practical *enough*," Nina went on. "You dream a lot, and you talk about freedom—but what are you going to do with it?"

"Anything I want."

"Like going to New York this summer? How will you support yourself? Are you going to try to be an actress? A model? Like a million other unhappy dreamers? Chances are you'll end up a waitress. Some dream."

Melanie spun the radio dial until she found a decent station. The thought of ending up like her mother almost made her panic. She didn't want to answer. Why was Nina putting her down? The whole idea of freedom was to give yourself choices. Narrow your vision too soon and you never realize your potential.

"Maybe I'll write a novel, or open a restaurant, or enter politics," Melanie said. "Whatever my dream is, I'll make it come true. The point is my life is just beginning. I'm eager to be independent. I'm not a coward like you. I don't need this tomb of a town. You act like you'd shrivel and die if you didn't have your parents or Billy approving of every move."

"And you don't need someone?" Nina jumped in. "You don't need a guy? You're totally self-sufficient?"

"That's right," Melanie lied, and turned the radio louder. She needed someone—a boyfriend—but she wanted more. It had to be real love—passion—not playacting like Nina's relationship with Billy.

Melanie thought of B.J. again. He was cute, fun, and he was going to be an Army officer. But for Melanie when things seemed too good to be true they usually were. Well this was one boy, she promised herself, that she wouldn't let get away. She loved that he listened to what she had to say. He seemed to accept her for what she was. Next weekend wouldn't come soon enough.

"I didn't mean to embarrass you tonight," Melanie apologized as they drove through Castroville's empty streets. "I just think you should put Billy into perspective. Even if you will marry him one day, that doesn't mean you can't go out on a blind date."

"If he finds out, he'll be really hurt," Nina offered. "I don't want to hurt him. He's never hurt me and he never will."

"Listen, if he can't understand what you're going through, what kind of boy is he?"

"You just don't like Billy," Nina said in frustration.

"Of course I like him. How can anyone not like Billy? He's thoughtful, kind, hard-working. I just wonder if he's right for you."

"Why?" Nina really wanted to know.

"Because he doesn't have your spirit, your imagination, your potential."

"Maybe," she admitted.

"He also acts like he owns you, Nina. Or you let him think that. Look how afraid you were to tell him you wanted to be free one night. You have to rebel once in a while. And don't worry, I bet your blind date turns out to be a dreamboat."

"That's enough," Nina said, tired. She couldn't believe how helpless she felt. Wanting the future but afraid to let go of the past. She remembered the cheap shot from that local reporter about how Nina had chosen Davis over Stanford and Berkeley, as if she wasn't thinking straight. What she hadn't told the woman or anyone else was how afraid she was of taking chances. She was afraid of challenges she might not be able to handle.

"You know what," she announced to Melanie, "you're right. I suppose I *am* a coward in some ways."

Melanie looked startled by the confession.

"But I'm going to change . . . I'm going to try anyway. I guess deep down I've wanted to for a while."

"Hip-hip," Melanie cheered.

"I'm just used to hanging on to the security I have. It's easy and I don't have to worry about anything. Being independent is too scary."

"But it's exciting, too. Just think, Nina—no one telling you who to be or what to do."

"Let's not go home yet," Nina suddenly ventured.

"What about getting back on time?"

"What about it?"

Melanie turned the car back toward Monterey and freedom. "Be honest," Melanie spoke up. "What did you think of B.J.?"

"I liked him. Do you think he's right for you?"

"Yes," Melanie said emphatically as she pressed her foot down. The car groaned its way to seventy, rattled like a tank, and shot down the highway. She loved the breeze, the canopy of stars, the ocean's roar. Everything felt wonderful.

They stopped at an all-night coffee shop and talked for hours. Old and new ideas began to swim in and out of focus for Nina. Maybe Melanie was right— Nina was living her life by what other people wanted. Billy and her parents practically kept her on a pedestal. The pressure to perform, to meet expectations, was too much. All anyone could do on a pedestal, Nina realized, was fall off. Well, she was going to do

62

what *she* wanted. This evening with Melanie had been a good choice after all.

It was pushing three when Melanie dropped Nina off at her house. Melanie called out a cheerful "bye" but Nina didn't look back. Her attention was on the light that had switched on in her parents' bedroom. In her nightgown, her mother peeked out from behind the curtain, the face furrowed in concern and disappointment. Nina knew there'd be questions, followed by a concerned lecture. She didn't want to hear it.

But what would she say? The courage and determination she'd found in the last few hours were already being challenged. She took a breath and marched up the walkway.

Life was becoming so complicated she suddenly wondered if it would ever be easy again.

8

❧★❧

"**W**ho's going to catch the most rats tonight?" Bradshaw boomed out in the darkness. A full moon hovered over the sergeant's shoulder. At parade rest, the forty trainees gazed reluctantly at the "hunting grounds" under the barracks. Cliff watched Bradshaw's eyes bore into him again, telling him that he was expected to lead the troops to victory. An order was an order, he thought. The argument in the barracks was whether Bradshaw was merely loony, had a load of money bet with the other drill sergeants, or was a card-carrying sadist. Cliff still wasn't sure—maybe all three were right on.

"Third Platoon's gonna catch the most rats, Sergeant!" came the chorus.

"Can't hear you, maggots—"

"THIRD PLATOON, SERGEANT!"

"Who?"

"THIRD PLATOON!!!!!!"

The hoarse voices squeaked out their allegiance to Bradshaw, even if most were dubious of the night's event. The sergeant had sweetened the pot by offering a prize for the trainee catching the most rats—an overnight weekend pass for two; for the squad hauling in the most booty, steak dinners in the mess hall. Cliff stole another glance at B.J. He looked eager, almost gung-ho. All week he'd eyed Cliff nervously, as if he couldn't believe Cliff hadn't told Bradshaw about the AWOL and the punch. Cliff finally confronted him and actually promised silence. It hadn't been an easy decision. Going AWOL couldn't be condoned, but Cliff had sympathized with B.J. for the unreasonable amount of punishment he'd endured. B.J. was grateful, yet when Cliff asked in a friendly way what B.J. had done in Monterey, he wouldn't tell him. Something had happened, Cliff guessed, because all week B.J. had been acting differently. In training he'd been trying harder, as if he now wanted to be an officer in the worst way.

"All right, scumbuckets, fall out. The hunt lasts till midnight. Any questions?"

The company clerk handed everyone the night's weapons: flashlight, pair of leather gloves, stick, gunnysack. Feet shuffled reluctantly toward the crawl space under the barracks.

"Hey, meathead," Bradshaw's voice rang out. Half the platoon turned. But it was B.J., who hadn't turned, who felt Bradshaw's hand on his shoulder. Cliff watched as the sergeant dropped him on the asphalt for fifty pushups.

"Meathead, I hope a rat bites your finger off,"
Bradshaw barked as B.J.'s face reddened.

"Yes, Sergeant."

"I hope it bites it off and you bleed to death, boy."

"Yes, Sergeant."

"You're a hopeless scumbag, Gibbons."

B.J. finally struggled up and joined the others under the barracks. Everyone crawled like lizards through the dirt, their flashlight beams crisscrossing aimlessly. In the darkness heads banged into the steel water pipes honeycombed overhead. Swirls of dust eddied up. Bodies collided.

"I can't breathe down here," someone spoke up.

"Love at first sight," came another voice as a flashlight caught the red, glinting eyes of the first rat. Large and fierce, standing on its hind legs, it glared insolently at the intruders.

Cliff overcame his squeamishness and lunged at a rat that skittered boldly near his legs. Its coat was wet and slimy. The sharp teeth dug into his gloved thumb, but he quickly capped his free hand over the head and wrestled the rat into his gunnysack. It shrieked like a child having a nightmare. Cliff kept hunting. Squirming through the dust he saw some of the other boys sneak out the crawl hole. He could hardly blame them. What surprised him was B.J. He was groping around as if on a life-or-death mission. A couple of rats were already his prisoners, dark, jumping bulges that gnawed at the burlap to escape.

As Cliff negotiated the darkness, he clanked his stick against the metal pipes, trying to ferret out the enemy. The rats grew more elusive by the minute, hiding in nooks in the floor joists. By ten minutes to midnight, he had captured thirteen. B.J. looked like he had bagged five or six, but he'd been struggling lately, coughing from the dust and continually wiping his eyes.

"Hey, Cliff," he whispered in the darkness, sidling up beside him.

Cliff looked at the blackened, exhausted face. "You okay?"

"I don't know, but I need to ask you a favor. A big favor."

Cliff studied him curiously.

"I'm not sure if you can understand this, but I *have* to get out of here next weekend. I have to win that pass—"

"What's so urgent?"

"I'm meeting someone. Someone special."

"Who?" Cliff said, annoyed by the secrecy. B.J. hadn't told him anything about his AWOL night, and here he was again with the cloak of mystery.

B.J. looked apologetic. "I can't tell you. Just believe me—I have to get out. Is there any way we could just trade gunnysacks?"

Cliff shook his head. "I can't do that."

"Why not?"

"Because it's wrong," Cliff allowed.

B.J. rubbed his eyes in frustration. "Come on. I'll level. I'm meeting a girl. I met her at a concert when I was AWOL. She's special. Really. We made a date for this weekend, a double date, in fact. You can come with me if you want. I'd like you to come with me . . ."

B.J. sounded desperate, but he was asking for the impossible. "I can't cheat," Cliff said.

"Give me a break," B.J. breathed. "I'll pay you back, I promise. You'll come with me. You'll meet a great girl."

Cliff was quiet.

"What skin is it off your nose? Do you want to win? Do you care about a pass?"

"No," he admitted. "I don't have anywhere special to go."

"Then help me."

Cliff turned away.

"You're something else," B.J. called out. "You're as cold-blooded as a fish! You're just like Bradshaw!"

A whistle shrilled from outside. The remaining hunters crawled out with their gunnysacks dragging behind them and joined the formation. Bradshaw collected the bags, gave them to the company clerk, who ran up to headquarters for an official count. Cliff knew he'd won individual "honors" for the platoon, but Bradshaw, angry, wanted to know why some boys hadn't caught anything. Didn't they care about the platoon's honor? he demanded. Frustrated, he called Cliff front and center of the formation. Placing a proud hand on his shoulder, Bradshaw announced, "Envy this man, maggots. He put you all to shame tonight. He's what the United States Army is all about. With pleasure I'll give him the weekend pass." He pulled a slip of paper from his pocket.

In the ranks there were sighs of resignation. B.J. gazed at the ground in defeat.

"Now, Weigel, who do you want to take with you?" Bradshaw asked, pen ready to fill in the name.

Cliff's eyes narrowed in indecision as they swept over his fellow trainees.

"You can go alone," Bradshaw allowed, as if to emphasize that no one but Cliff really deserved a free weekend.

"Sergeant, I choose Private Gibbons."

Cliff's voice crashed the silence like a hydrogen bomb. Bradshaw stared at him.

"Say again, boy?"

"Private Gibbons, Sergeant Bradshaw."

The sergeant rocked back on his heels, as if he wasn't understanding. "Who?"

"Private Gibbons, Sergeant."

B.J. wanted to drop on his knees in adoration before Cliff. The guy's heart wasn't made of stone after all. But his rush of elation began to ebb. B.J. didn't have to look at Bradshaw to feel the sergeant's growing revulsion.

"Is this a joke, Private Weigel?"

"No, Sergeant."

"You really want to take this lowly maggot with you?"

"Yes, Sergeant."

"Why?"

"I have my reasons."

Bradshaw looked stunned, uncomprehending. B.J. knew that underneath the shock was a smoldering volcano. Embarrassed by Cliff's selection, Bradshaw was trying to control himself. His eyes traveled up from the ground to focus not on B.J., but on Cliff. Then he walked a desultory circle around the platoon's top trainee.

"You surely must be tired," Bradshaw said to Cliff. "Your brain isn't clear. You aren't thinking."

"I'm thinking fine, Sergeant. You said it was to be a two-man pass. And that the winner could take anyone he wanted."

"That's what I said, all right. What I didn't say was that Maggot Gibbons couldn't go. So why don't you choose somebody else?"

"But, Sergeant, I picked Private Gibbons. There were no other rules."

In that agonizing moment no one so much as twitched. B.J. felt a cold rush to his heart.

"I'm giving you one more chance, Weigel." Bradshaw stood inches from the trainee's unyielding face. "Do yourself a favor—I take your choice of Gibbons as a personal insult. Do you want to insult me?"

"No, Sergeant. But I'm not changing my mind."

No one could doubt Cliff's courage, B.J. thought, but it sure didn't make sense. Cliff was throwing away his privileged position in the platoon, and maybe his future as an officer. No one should have messed with Bradshaw.

"Then Private Gibbons it is," Bradshaw said in a voice that would have chilled the warmest heart. The conciliatory gesture fooled no one as he scribbled B.J.'s name on the pass with Cliff's and handed it over. Bradshaw retreated to the NCO quarters.

Exhausted, everyone fell out to the barracks. B.J. started to approach Cliff to thank him, but Cliff walked quickly away, as if he were thinking about what he'd done.

B.J. waited till everyone was asleep before pulling

out his writing pad. He ducked into the latrine and turned on the bare bulb overhead.

Hey, Bobby,

It's almost 1:00 A.M. and I can't sleep. I do this a lot, actually—hang out in the latrine and write letters at crazy hours. Especially after crazy days. Would you believe it if I told you we were up till midnight trying to catch rats with flashlights and gunnysacks? Scout's honor. But even crazier things have happened to me. I met this wonderful girl at a rock concert in Monterey Friday night. I know you're not supposed to meet girls while slaving away through basic training, but I managed to get free for the night. Now Melanie and I have a date next weekend. I owe that good fortune in part to a fellow trainee named Cliff Weigel. You see, Cliff caught the most rats tonight and was rewarded with a weekend pass for two, which he's generously sharing with yours truly. If you're confused by now, let me admit that I am a little, too. I mean, sometimes I feel another B.J. is going through the Army and I'm just watching him, wondering what will happen next. I wish I could tell you more about Cliff. You'd like him. He's as interesting as he is unusual. I think I'm going to be knowing him a little better . . .

The pen froze in B.J.'s hand as his ear caught footsteps in the barracks. He rushed to turn off the light but Bradshaw was already standing at the latrine threshold. B.J. took a step back, expecting the worst as their eyes met. After a long moment the sergeant only turned and headed back outside. Bradshaw's eyes said it all. *If he or Cliff thought basic training had been tough so far, wait for the weeks to come . . .*

9

In their dress greens and polished black shoes, Cliff and B.J. stood outside the Fort Ord entrance and pushed out their thumbs in the direction of Monterey. Part of Cliff wished he were back in the barracks, sleeping. Even after a long shower he ached from the torture Bradshaw had begun to put him through all week. He'd sensed that when he'd challenged the sergeant about the pass things might become more difficult, but he never imagined this. Wherever he walked on the company street the drill sergeants dropped him for pushups. Every night he was ordered to run laps around the barracks until his legs burned. Twice he'd been assigned to guard a deserted rifle range on a freezing night without his jacket. This morning, Bradshaw had called him out of formation with a personal message. "You can kiss off OCS, boy. You're going to be drummed out of the corps before you get there. I promise you, you can't beat me or the Army. It's against the rules, like someone trying to steal first base. Other trainees before you have tried and always failed. I've made this our private war, Private, and you're going to lose. You read me, Weigel?"

Loud and clear. But if Bradshaw expected him to apologize, or give back the pass, Cliff thought the sergeant could die holding his breath. Cliff had been loyal to B.J. not only out of sympathy but also because he had the right to choose anyone he wanted. Maybe he'd been proving to everybody that he was his own man, but it boiled down to being a matter of principle. You just didn't go back on your word, as Bradshaw had tried to do. Cliff believed in the importance of having his own values and sticking to them. His mother taught him early on that his father wanted him to live by his honesty and integrity. That was his birthright from his father.

Cliff had an image of his father that he cherished and which always gave him courage. He knew now that he'd need that courage more than ever. This bully of a sergeant wasn't going to beat him in a war of wills. Cliff promised himself he would stand up to everything in Bradshaw's arsenal. He was going to end up an officer. That had always been his dream, and no one was going to take it away. The Army wasn't made up entirely of Bradshaws. The sergeant was the rotten apple hidden in the bunch.

A car pulled onto the highway shoulder and Cliff and B.J. gratefully got in. The driver was headed close enough to their rendezvous to make the evening start off right.

"I can't believe it," B.J. marveled. "We're actually free."

"For the night anyway," Cliff amended.

B.J. looked at his friend. He was sorry for what Cliff had endured all week. Bradshaw had slightly given up picking on B.J. His main target now was Cliff. B.J. couldn't help but feel a little guilty about the switch. "Let's be glad we're out of the Army, even for a night," B.J. said to rally his friend's spirits. "We're going to have a great time. Your date's gorgeous."

Cliff couldn't remember the last time he'd had a blind date. He'd never dated much, period. Two summers ago he'd met a pretty brunette at a taco stand where he'd worked and had a short summer romance. Wrapped up in herself, the girl had never really paid much attention to Cliff. She just wanted to have a good time. Cliff had never given much thought to falling in love, getting crazy over a girl. He'd always focused on his future career as an officer. He'd assumed that once he got his commission he'd probably settle down—find someone to marry and raise a family—but he wasn't counting the days.

"There they are," B.J. called out, pointing to two silhouettes in an old Chevy convertible. The driver stopped, and Cliff scurried after B.J. across the highway to a parking lot. He waited as B.J. approached a girl with reddish curly hair. Her face lit up when she saw him.

"Hey, Cliff, come over here," B.J. called with a wave. "I want you to meet Melanie and Nina.

As B.J. introduced him Cliff's eyes swam to the blonde who was his blind date. B.J. was right, Nina was a real looker. He'd always liked blondes, and Nina's body was exceptional. But she didn't act so impressed with him. Her hand played nervously with her necklace.

"I think I know you," Nina finally said to Cliff.

Cliff squinted back uncertainly.

"Oh, how could you?" echoed Melanie, and acted embarrassed.

"He helped us change our flat tire, in front of Fort Ord," Nina explained to B.J.

Cliff remembered hazily. His mother had been driving him over from the induction center in San Francisco. While the other inductees had all been shepherded into an Army bus to Fort Ord, Cliff's mother, feeling protective, convinced him to go with her in their car. He'd almost felt embarrassed but he didn't want to argue with her. At only seventeen, just like B.J., he had needed parental written permission before he could enlist.

"Well, where shall we go?" Melanie chimed in.

"What about San Francisco?"

It was B.J.'s suggestion. Melanie looked eager. "Terrific," she said. "Does everybody like to dance? I know an old-fashioned ballroom near Chinatown. There's not much of a cover to get in. It'll be like an old Army movie. Dancing with our soldiers before they go off to war."

They climbed into the convertible, Cliff and Nina in back. "Well, we're not up for war, but let's dance!" B.J. said as he turned the ignition key. "Cliff, old buddy, got your dancing shoes on?"

"Sure," he said, though he wasn't a great dancer. He didn't say there were different kinds of war, but he couldn't help but think it. He looked at Nina, who nodded okay.

The car squealed onto the highway toward San Francisco. Melanie kept the ragtop down and the radio up. Nina looked annoyed or disappointed about something, and despite the earlier ice-breaker, Cliff felt she was cool toward him. He tried to talk to her—about the Army, high school, the last couple of movies he'd seen—but no matter how polite he was Nina didn't seem to respond. Was she disappointed in him as a date? Was he supposed to be more witty? Maybe she wanted to be with someone else tonight.

The Chevy lurched up and down the steep hills of San Francisco, dodging cable cars and pedestrians, each stomach-flipping rise bringing a *whoop* from Melanie. She directed B.J. through Chinatown and down a narrow street of arty movie houses, ethnic restaurants, and renovated warehouse lofts. The ballroom was on the second floor of a former firehouse. The brass pole, shiny as a mirror, was the only remnant of the past. Victorian wallpaper added a feeling of elegance, the floor was inlaid parquet, and a full orchestra played a waltz for a couple of hundred people dressed in everything from tuxedos to parachute pants.

"Isn't this place wild?" said Melanie, looking around. "I love it. Dance with me, sir?" she said to B.J.

Cliff watched them head out, arm in arm, then asked Nina if she wanted to dance. With a slight smile she said she'd twisted her ankle while riding a bike, and she'd prefer just to sit out the first few. Cliff was sure it was a lie, and that Nina had to know that he knew. Didn't she care? He escorted her to one of the small glass tables that bordered the floor and ordered two beers. Nina hardly touched hers. "Would you like something else?" he asked. She said no, and fixed an exasperated gaze on Melanie as she whirled with B.J. in a dizzying waltz. Cliff ordered a second beer. What was with this girl, anyway? Looking at Nina told him she was smart and probably from a nice home. He wouldn't mind getting to know her. Maybe he'd missed out not having a real girlfriend. But this ice cube was too hard to crack.

"Is there some reason," Cliff suddenly asked in frustration, "why you're so angry?" The words popped out, like when he'd challenged Bradshaw.

Nina stared at the handsome, square-shouldered boy. What had he just said? For the last hour she had been silently cursing Melanie for sticking her with a boy who was almost a perfect clone for Billy. Polite, gracious, and about as exciting and imaginative as a postage stamp. This was liberating? This was her dreamboat? She had argued a solid hour with her mother to defend her right to go out with someone besides Billy, and look what she'd come up with. All she wanted was for the night to end as painlessly as possible so she could go home. But apparently Cliff didn't see it that way. He had a big mouth. She knew Billy would never have said anything like that.

"If you don't like my company," Nina said, "why don't you find someone else to sit with?"

"Fine . . . if that'll make you any happier . . ."

"Yes it would."

"You know," Cliff added as he stood, "maybe I'm not your idea of a great date, but you could at least be civil."

Nina suddenly felt bad. He was right, she hadn't

been fair. "Maybe it's not you," she answered. "Maybe I've got something else on my mind."

"Like what?"

"Look," she explained, "I didn't even want to go out tonight."

"How was I supposed to know? If you were miserable, you should have gone home. I would have taken you."

Nina sighed and tried to compose herself. "I'm sorry. Sit down if you want. You really do seem like a nice person."

She picked up her beer finally and turned her gaze to the dance floor. She was still surprised by Cliff's frankness. There was a spark to him after all, and maybe potential fire. He was different from Billy. She turned to tell him that she wouldn't mind dancing after all when the orchestra stopped. A swell of angry voices took the place of the music.

Oh no, Nina thought, as she focused on Melanie. Ringed by spectators in the middle of the dance floor, she was glaring at some heavy-metal type in leather jeans and a chain belt. He'd asked Melanie to dance, Nina gathered, and she had refused in her usual direct way. The boy's friends, tall and rangy with sullen faces, crowded around B.J.

"Hey, soldier boy," someone taunted him, "your girl's sure got bad taste."

B.J. pulled back his arm and launched a missile. Nina shuddered as the smart-ass recoiled lifelessly to the floor. Glancing at his fist in surprise and triumph, B.J. was blind to the others. Before he could move they drowned him in swinging arms and legs.

"Wait here," Cliff said to Nina.

Like the heroine she always wanted to be, Melanie tried to break through the maze of bodies to rescue B.J. Nina looked on helplessly. Cliff reached the fight and gently pushed Melanie away, then pulled off the attackers two at a time, trying to duck their wild punches. Cliff was strong and capable, Nina saw, and she wondered why he didn't hit anyone back. They were really trying to cream him. He finally seized B.J. by the arm and jerked him free of the melee. Nina grabbed Melanie and hurried out after them.

Safe on the street, a shaken B.J. thanked Cliff and retreated into the car with Melanie. Nina took a closer look at Cliff. A deep gash ran from his lip down to his chin. "Here," she said, concerned, and pulled a handkerchief from her purse.

Cliff shook his head. "I'll be okay."

"Don't be so stubborn." She pushed the handkerchief against the wound. She could make out some swelling under his eye, too. The fighting had been worse than she'd realized. "Get into the car and I can take a better look," she offered.

"I'd rather take a walk with you."

She glanced squeamishly at the cut again. At least the bleeding had stopped. "Okay," she said, and pushed her arm through Cliff's. There was something about him she liked. Maybe it was keeping his head during the fight. He was more mature than most boys at school.

"I want you to know I'm sorry again for tonight," Nina said. "I don't know what got into me."

"It's okay. I wasn't in a great mood myself." He looked at her. "Have you got a steady boyfriend?"

"What?"

80

"I was wondering why you were so cool to me. A boyfriend would explain it."

She laughed, surprised by Cliff's intuition. "I do," she admitted, "only Melanie thinks he's not right for me. That's the reason for our date tonight. You're supposed to be the answer to the prayers I haven't said yet. Does that make sense?"

"I think so."

"I hope so." She wondered if Cliff knew that she liked him. "Are you in B.J.'s platoon?"

Cliff nodded. "We're going to Officer Candidate School together."

"Melanie's crazy about anyone in the Army," Nina allowed, "especially officers. She thinks B.J.'s the living end, in case you haven't noticed. Me, I don't know anything about the military, even if I've lived near Fort Ord all my life."

"That's Castroville?" Cliff said, remembering the conversation when he'd changed the tire. "It's funny, I've never lived in one spot more than a couple of years. My mother was always moving us around."

"How long have you wanted to be in the Army?" she asked.

"Forever. Do you think that's strange? Kids today don't want anything to do with the Army."

"I don't think so," she said. "You must have had a good reason for enlisting."

"My father was an infantry captain in Vietnam. Six days before he was to come home, he was killed in a firefight near Khe Sanh."

"Oh, I'm sorry," she said.

"Do you know anything about the Vietnam War?"

81

"A little from history class. No one liked it, I know that."

"No one liked the war," Cliff echoed, "and everyone forgot about the soldiers who fought in it. I couldn't forget my father. I barely knew him, yet I still miss him. I feel a loyalty to him. I always wanted to follow in his footsteps."

"What did your mother say about that?"

"Part of her was afraid she'd lose a son the way she lost a husband. But she was also proud that I was following my father's path."

Nina could see pride and defiance in Cliff's face. "At least you know what you want to do with your life," she said.

"How about you?" he asked.

Nina made a playful face. "I'm *supposed* to know what I'm doing. Everyone thinks I do. The truth is I'm really up in the air. It's a boring story."

"Tell me."

"There's not much to tell. Everyone has great expectations for me. I don't know if I can meet them. People act like I'm perfect, but the truth is I have a lot of doubts about myself. You have no idea what that pressure is like."

"I've a little. The Army has certain expectations. And I've got some for myself. I want to live up to them."

"I'm not sure that I do," Nina volunteered as they strolled down the street. It felt so good to be out with someone besides Billy, she thought. With Cliff she wasn't reminded of her image as a golden girl or her responsibility of living up to it. For tonight at least she was someone else, and without a past she could

82

enjoy the present. She could also better understand Melanie's feelings. Freedom really was intoxicating.

Nina's eyes jumped to Cliff and she decided to be brave. "Am I ever going to see you again?"

He seemed pleased that she'd asked, but after a moment she saw disappointment in his eyes. "Not for another four weeks, at least," he said. "That's when I graduate from basic. If I do it on time," he added.

"What do you mean?"

"My sergeant isn't overly fond of me."

"Why?" It was hard to believe anyone not liking Cliff. Nina knew he had to be a conscientious soldier.

"It's Sergeant Bradshaw's problem. He's a bully, and a rotten apple, too. But I'll survive him."

"Are you sure you can't get another pass?"

Cliff said it was impossible, he was stuck in basic. And after basic he might be transferred immediately to another fort without a leave. Nina searched his face to see if it were true, or if Cliff just didn't want to see her again. She wanted to see him. He took her out of her small world and gave her a fresh perspective. She thought he was the most interesting boy she'd ever met.

On the way home, Nina didn't mind when Melanie put the top down. The cold air gave her an excuse to move next to Cliff and rest her head on his shoulder. She didn't want the night to end.

The four stopped for coffee at a diner, then drove back to the fort while B.J. and Melanie sang to the radio. It was after two when they stopped at the entrance. An ocean fog had rolled in, and a lone floodlight shone eerily on the MP on duty. Melanie and B.J. locked in an embrace that Nina registered as a "10."

Melanie vowed to see B.J. next weekend, though after what Cliff had said about basic training and Sergeant Bradshaw, Nina didn't see how.

Nina slid out of the car to say goodbye. But as her eyes glided to Cliff just a goodbye didn't seem enough. She felt a little foolish and vulnerable as she moved toward him. She'd never been this forward with Billy. Go on, make things happen for yourself, she thought. She forgot her self-consciousness and pressed her lips against Cliff's. His arms circled her shoulders. She didn't want him to let go. When the kiss finally ended she felt cheated somehow. She knew she would have to see her soldier again.

B.J. watched the taillights of Melanie's car blur and fade into the foggy blackness. Six hours of being in heaven, and now he had to return to prison . . . He showed his pass to the MP and marched with Cliff down the dark road to their company street.

"Now I know what it means to be depressed," B.J. tried to joke. "Part of me wants to turn around and head out of here—and never come back."

"Why?" asked Cliff.

"Why? Because I want my freedom."

"If you want it so much, why did you ever enlist?"

B.J. gave Cliff an appraising look. He thought of manufacturing another lie, but he sensed he couldn't fool Cliff, and suddenly he didn't want to either. He had to stop putting up a facade, stop trying to hide his fears, not just from others but himself. "I enlisted because I was a big success in high school, but a flop in college," he said after a moment. "There was nothing to do but enlist. I felt like a failure. I wish I could be sure I was going to make it in the Army."

Cliff gave him a pat on the shoulder. "You'll do fine, B.J."

"You think so?"

"Just believe in yourself. Anyway, Bradshaw's off your back and on mine now."

"A small miracle," B.J. said.

"Anyway, what would happen if you got out of the Army and couldn't find anything to do?"

There was such sincerity in Cliff's voice, and a perspective to his thinking, that B.J. believed him. Between Cliff and Melanie he couldn't miss, he suddenly thought. He felt a surge of hope. Melanie had promised to see him again, somehow ferreting her way onto the post. It would be difficult but Melanie could do it if anyone could. The girl was really gutsy, and she inspired B.J.'s own courage. He'd never have taken a swing at those gorillas tonight if he hadn't felt that Melanie expected and deserved it.

"Did you have a good time tonight?" B.J. asked Cliff in the silence. "I thought Nina really liked you. Didn't I tell you she was gorgeous?" He wanted Cliff to say something, wanted him to admit he'd had a good time, because B.J. owed that to him at least. But Cliff was back to his quiet, private self. B.J. wondered again why Cliff hadn't fought back on the dance floor. Maybe he didn't need to prove himself, he thought, unlike B.J.

Except for a lone light from the NCO barracks, Charlie Company street was dark and lifeless. Cliff said goodnight to B.J. and slumped wearily on his bunk. He tried not to think about Nina anymore. He'd enjoyed the date more than he'd anticipated, especially the goodnight kiss. He could still smell her perfume. She was the kind of girl he could really go for, and she had liked him. But now the good times were over. He had to concentrate on surviving basic. He wasn't sure how difficult that would be with Bradshaw on his case, how he would react to more punishment. He could give B.J. perfect advice but had no idea what to do himself.

Like B.J., Cliff thought, he had his insecurities, too. Loneliness washed over him as he undressed. It was a feeling he'd had before, that came and went without warning. Something to do with growing up without a father, he always thought. There had been a void in his life, so he had conjured up an image of a man who was kind and honest and loving. But as special as the image was, it never felt like enough. Cliff had been cheated without knowing quite who to blame or what to do about it. If he could just succeed in the Army, he thought, maybe the void would close up and disappear.

All that stood in his way was Bradshaw.

Shivering, Cliff threw back his blanket and crawled under, grateful for the chance to sleep. At least the nights were his own. Something warm and slimy suddenly brushed his leg. He turned over and sat up. A fierce pain dug into his ankle and spiraled up his leg. In desperation he tumbled to the floor.

On the exposed sheet a scruffy rat glared back haughtily. Jesus, he thought. Disquieted, Cliff studied the pugnacious face. It reminded him of the drill sergeant who he felt certain had put the rat there.

10

⌐★⌐

"Billy, stop," Nina said, annoyed when he tried to kiss her again. On this overcast Sunday morning, they sat in his pickup in front of Nina's house, ready for church. "Someone's going to see us . . ."

"So what?" he answered, annoyed. "Everyone knows us. And who cares if it's Sunday? Remember the church picnic last year?"

"Yes," she said, suddenly laughing. "You tore your jeans on the barbed-wire fence. Up to then, it was very romantic."

"Hey, it was a good time. Admit it."

She let him kiss her. "I agree."

"And lots more to come."

"That would be nice."

"I love you, Nina."

For a moment she felt happy and secure in his arms, as she had so many times. She liked Billy's easygoing style, his concern for her. And he looked incredibly handsome. If he didn't want to farm, he could have been a male model, she liked to think. The doe-brown eyes were intense and sincere.

"Penny for your thoughts," she said, dropping her head on his shoulder.

"My thoughts? They're about you."

"Elaborate, please."

"Well, right now I feel everything is great between us. Perfect maybe. But the last couple of weeks, I haven't been so sure."

"What's been different?"

"You."

"Me?" she said with mock amazement.

"You've been keeping to yourself."

"I've been busy with school, that's all."

"What about last weekend? You went out with Melanie and wouldn't tell me anything. What's the big deal?"

"Nothing," she swore. "You don't have to know *everything* I do. I'm not always prying into your life, am I?"

"I wish you would. Sometimes I feel you don't care anymore."

Nina glanced back to her house. Her mother and father were getting into their car, and they gave her a half wave. Nina had sworn her mother to secrecy about the concert two weeks ago. She hadn't been pleased that Nina had not been honest with Billy. The date in San Francisco Nina had kept top secret. She wasn't ready to tell anybody about Cliff. She wanted to see him again before she made up her mind to drop bombshells on the home front.

"Billy, I don't think I feel up to church today," Nina

volunteered. It was supposed to sound spontaneous, but she felt self-conscious.

"What's the matter?"

"I don't feel like going, that's all. I've got a headache, and I have a lot of homework due Monday. I think I should stay home. You go ahead . . ."

"No," he said, suspicious.

"Billy, please?" She gave him a kiss and climbed out of the pickup. "I'll be okay. Go on, I'll see you soon." She half-expected him to follow her into her house, but after a moment he drove off. Nina had dropped onto her bed when the doorbell rang. Melanie let herself in, a wide smile pasted on her face.

"Okay," she announced cheerfully in Nina's room, "I'm glad you decided to stay home. We're calling today Operation REBEL."

Nina chuckled. "What, pray tell, does that mean?"

"*Rescue Behind Enemy Lines*. Look here—" Melanie held up Defense Department pamphlet DD-214-71: Rules and Regulations for Civilian Visitation of Domestic Military Installations.

"Where did you get that?"

"The Army recruiting office in Monterey. I told them I was doing an article on Fort Ord for the school paper. May I quote now?"

"Please," said Nina, applauding.

"Page twenty-seven, paragraph three, subparagraph two, section b: '*Any immediate family member of a basic trainee is entitled to visit said trainee but only at the discretion of the officer or noncommissioned officer in charge, and providing that no military or training activities are scheduled or anticipated to be scheduled at the time of said visit . . .*'"

"What gobbledegook," Nina interjected.

"That's just Army talk. The point is this is Sunday, right? Even trainees have Sunday off. Ergo, no military activities. B.J. told me some families have already visited some of the guys."

"But we're not immediate family."

"Who says? How would his sergeant know I'm not B.J.'s wife, or you're not his sister?" On cue, Melanie pulled her mother's wedding band from a skirt pocket and slipped it on her left hand. "Mom doesn't wear it anymore, not after the divorce. Why not put it to good use?"

"But you look too young to be married."

"I'll put on makeup."

"I still don't know," Nina said. "According to Cliff, Bradshaw is real tough."

"Well, so am I," Melanie said positively. "Listen, it was your idea, too, that we see them today. Are you with me or not?" Melanie suddenly fixed on the pillow she was half-lying on. She smiled impishly as she shoved it under her loose-fitting blouse. "Now what sergeant, even if he's tougher than horsemeat, is going to deny a pregnant wife a visit?"

"Okay," said Nina, surrendering to her friend's audacity.

"Once we're in Charlie Company, you can sneak off and find Cliff," Melanie said. "Don't worry. This will go smooth as butter."

As Melanie's Chevy roared down Castroville's quiet Sunday streets, Nina thought of a dozen *what-ifs*. What if the MP wouldn't even let them through the main gate? What if B.J. or Cliff wasn't with his platoon? What if Sergeant Bradshaw saw through their charade—would they all get into trouble? No, everything would be fine. She always worried too much. They reached the main gate around ten-thirty, falling in in the long line of visitors' cars. On Sunday even the MP offered a smile as they approached.

"Excuse me, which way to Charlie Company, Second Battalion, Third Brigade?" Melanie asked him sweetly.

The directions were rattled off. "Got that?" Melanie said blithely to Nina, and zoomed ahead. "Golly, look at this place," she said as they drove through the small city, "it's something else."

"Like another planet," Nina seconded. She studied the mirror-image rows of two-story barracks, pale green prehistoric structures that had to be depressing to live in. Around the PX were bored-looking soldiers. A block away, a few lost souls stood outside a church that looked like an ordinary barracks. Zombie City. Nina felt sorry for B.J. and Cliff. The car glided up a steep hill and turned right. The Second Battalion rested on a crown that allowed a partial view of the ocean. They found Charlie Company and parked. Nearby, several trainees sat on the grass with wives or parents.

"See?" said Melanie, adjusting her pillow. "Families, just like us."

"Lead on, fearless mother."

Lead on she would, thought Melanie, as she approached a stray soldier. "Can you tell me where I can find my husband, B.J. Gibbons, please?" Melanie was directed to the day officer in the company headquarters. She didn't mind the whistles and catcalls that followed them from barracks doors, but she could see Nina was embarrassed. Inside headquarters they found several empty desks, rifles padlocked in a corner stand, and a bulletin board with a faded, dog-eared Red Cross poster. Voices drifted out from behind a closed door.

"Go ahead, knock," Nina whispered.

Melanie hovered closer, listening. A poker game, she thought. She remembered eavesdropping on her father's Saturday-night games, smelling the cigars and stale beer and hearing the plastic chips slide over the velvet cloth. Laughter suddenly erupted from behind the door.

Melanie knocked firmly.

The door squeaked open. A boyish face peered at her hazily. After B.J.'s description, she would have known Sergeant Bradshaw anywhere. There was liquor on his breath.

"Hello, I'm B.J. Gibbons' wife, and I've just flown in from Pittsburgh with his sister—"

Melanie held her breath. Bradshaw's glance flicked to Nina and back to Melanie as she rested her hands on her belly. He couldn't be putting two and two together, she thought suddenly—B.J. and Cliff on leave last weekend, and suddenly a *wife* and *sister* show up? Would he check personnel records to see if B.J. was really married? Bradshaw's eyes remained unfocused. Sniffling, he ran a finger under his nose as he retrieved a clipboard. Both girls signed in their phony names.

"Visiting hours are over at noon," he said distantly. "Your boy Gibbons is in the first barracks on your left."

Outside, Nina went to find Cliff as Melanie ducked

92

into B.J.'s barracks. She found him in his fatigues by his bunk, polishing his boots. He glanced up at a pregnant woman with heavily rouged cheeks.

"Don't just sit there gawking," whispered Melanie.

B.J. focused again. "Is that you—?"

"We haven't got long," Melanie said, and grabbed him by the hand. They escaped to a visitors' picnic table out of view of wandering trainees. Melanie was giddy that her plan had worked, but she was even more excited to be alone with B.J. Even though they'd been together only twice, she felt she knew him well. They were fated for one another. Nina might call her a hopeless romantic, but Melanie knew her heart.

She got rid of the pillow and they fell into each other's arms.

"Are things okay?" she asked.

"I guess," he said cautiously. "With three weeks to graduation I'm starting to hope." He rapped his knuckles on the table.

"That's exciting. But you always knew you'd make it . . ."

He arched his head to the sun, half-closing his eyes in deliberation before looking back at Melanie. "You want the truth?" he said. "I told Cliff. I owe it to you, too. When I first met you, Melanie, I didn't know if I would make it. I lied to you at the concert. I really had all kinds of doubts. I didn't do well in college, and I didn't start out well in the Army . . ."

"You lied to me?" she said, a little hurt.

"I'm sorry. I'd put a lot of pressure on myself. But you changed that for me."

"What do you mean?"

"You were so up, and gutsy. It inspired me."

Melanie felt better, even pleased. Most boys she'd dated acted so self-sufficient, too proud to admit to any weakness or that they might need help. B.J. was just the opposite. He needed somebody. He needed her. "What is it?" she asked when she caught him looking unhappy.

"Just thinking about Cliff. Bradshaw's really after him. He expects Cliff to give up, but Cliff won't. It's like an irresistible force meeting an immovable object. I don't know what's going to happen. Cliff won't talk to anyone, not even me. I worry about him in his shell."

"He'll be all right," Melanie said. She hardly knew Cliff but he seemed extremely capable. She let her hand graze B.J.'s cheek. "I've really missed you. I want to see you again next Sunday."

"That would be great."

"Can I bring you something? Food? Some books?"

"Just yourself."

"B.J.—"

He looked at her.

"What's going to happen when you graduate? I mean, I know you go on to more training, then Officer Candidate School—but do you get a leave after basic?"

"I don't know. Maybe I can request one. I want to be with you."

"Really?" She needed to be reassured. Just when she fell for the right boy, and he fell for her, she didn't want fate to mess things up. She wouldn't let that happen.

"I think about you all the time," he said. "That's how I get by every day. Do you think about me?"

"Yes," she admitted, embracing him again. She sat in his arms and watched as the sun drifted behind the clouds, then laid her head on his chest. When B.J. stirred she made him lie still. "Quiet," she whispered. "I'm listening to your heart."

For five minutes Nina had traveled from barracks to barracks, drawing wry smiles and more whistles before someone told her Cliff Weigel was on KP. Uncertain, she peeked into the cavernous mess hall with its rows of empty tables and bright stainless steel counters.

"Cliff?" she called timidly.

Something stirred in the back of the kitchen. A head finally peeked up. She strained to recognize Cliff. His cheek was black and blue and a crescent-shaped gash was stamped on his neck like a tattoo. A puffy lip made him look clownish.

"What happened to you?" she said, appalled.

Cliff had his sleeves rolled up, cutting tops off carrots. He gazed at Nina, not quite believing it was her. "Sergeant Bradshaw," he finally said.

"Are you all right?" Nina sat beside him when he dropped on a bench. Cliff didn't say anything. He seemed closed, guarded. Nina explained about Melanie's crazy scheme to meet B.J. today, that she'd come along for fun. No, not really, she admitted only to herself. She'd come to see Cliff because she missed him. Nina couldn't find the nerve to tell him she wanted to see more of him, and to make him part of her life.

"I don't know how I am, if you want the truth," he suddenly opened up.

"How did it happen?" she said, glancing at his face.

"Bradshaw hit me with a rifle butt."

"But why?"

"Because I insulted him. Because I stand up to him. The man's a lunatic," Cliff said. "Everyone knows and expects basic training to be drudgery, but it's not supposed to be punitive. I keep wondering what my father would do if he were in my place."

"And?" Nina asked.

"Sometimes I think he'd clobber Bradshaw. Other times I'm sure he'd do what I'm doing . . . turn the other cheek, gut it out. I've never believed in fistfights, not unless you're really in trouble. Wars are bad enough without fighting when you don't have to." He looked at Nina. "Anyway, all I have to do is last a couple more weeks."

"But what if he beats you up some more? Do you think he will?"

"Probably."

"Can't you talk to him or someone else? Work things out?" Nina said. "In school—"

"This isn't school."

"You could still talk to him."

"Only if I told him I was backing down. I won't do that."

"Then go to your commanding officer and complain," she suggested. Nina only wanted to help.

"How many trainees complain to their CO every day? Trainees always complain, it's their nature, like it's the CO's nature not to believe them. And if I ever protested, Bradshaw would probably find out. Things would get worse."

"You have to do something," Nina said, feeling as frustrated as Cliff.

"Thanks for the concern," he said, "but there's nothing you can do."

"Yes I can. I could talk to somebody at Fort Ord. I know I'm not your relative, but I live nearby, I can tell them how badly you've been hurt. I'm part of this community, my word should mean something—"

"That's naive," he said, and turned away.

Nina knew she'd said the wrong thing. She was trying to be supportive because she cared for Cliff. She didn't know if he turned away because he didn't want her help or if it was his pride. The silence felt awkward.

"I better get back to work," Cliff finally said.

The cool voice chilled her. Nina didn't get it. Cliff had started to open up to her, and now he was being a clam. Didn't he care how beat up he got?

"You've lost perspective," Nina spoke up. "Someone beat you up and you think you're being a hero by not complaining. You're really just playing it safe. You have to take some risks when something goes wrong."

"What do you know about risks?" he said sharply.

"Coming here was a risk for me. Going out last weekend was, too. If you knew my family you'd understand. But I'm glad I did it, no matter what the consequences."

Cliff turned quiet again, caught up in his own problems. Nina suddenly regretted coming today. She'd been hopeful of a new relationship, but maybe Cliff didn't want one.

"I think I better go," she said, standing.

Cliff looked up apologetically. He couldn't tell her how he was feeling. He hadn't meant to be cold, but no one, including Nina, had any idea what he was going through. She couldn't help him; no one could. Last week had been a nightmare, worse than anything B.J. had ever endured. Bradshaw had made Cliff eat his meals in sixty seconds, low crawl in his underwear around the barracks in the middle of the night, go through the tear-gas chamber without a mask until he puked for hours. Then the sergeant had clobbered him with the rifle butt in hand-to-hand combat with a smile on his face. How could Cliff think about anything but survival with his shoulders pinned to the ground? Somehow no one else saw or did anything about Bradshaw's behavior. It was hard for Cliff to reach out to Nina when he saw all his dreams slipping away.

"Well, goodbye," Nina said, still lingering.

Did she want him to kiss her? Part of Cliff wished she would stay, but what was the point? He was too tired, too frustrated. Helplessly he watched her march out of the mess hall, wondering if he'd ever see her again.

11

"You look a little pale around the gills," Melanie observed as the car streamed out of Fort Ord to the highway.

"I'm still in shock," Nina admitted. "He wasn't the same Cliff." Nina had told Melanie all about Cliff's problems with Bradshaw. What Nina hadn't detailed was how ambivalent Cliff had acted toward her. Did he really like her or not? She could understand his siege mentality, but didn't Cliff realize it wasn't just him against the world? She was on his side, too.

It was almost one when Melanie dropped Nina at her house and she hurried up the brick walkway, wanting to beat her parents back from church. She was startled to smell cookies baking.

"Nina—"

She turned to face her mother. Her father was in the living room. On the couch Billy sat looking morose. Was this a wake?

"Hi," she said after a beat. Her heart was a jack-hammer.

"Honey, where were you?" her mother asked. Her expression said she already knew the answer wouldn't be good news.

"Just out," Nina answered quietly, looking at Billy.

"You told Billy you had a headache."

"I wanted some fresh air."

"Come help me in the kitchen."

Nina managed a smile and followed.

"I just called Melanie's mother. She said Melanie's been seeing some soldier in basic training. And you two had a double date last weekend. She's sure you went to Fort Ord this morning—"

"Mother, *please* . . ." Nina's face colored. How could her mother be saying this.

"Now what's going on?" her mother demanded.

Nina looked at her mother's lovely face. It was proud, but now Nina also saw deep concern and confusion. Her golden daughter was up to something that was inexplicable and inexcusable. That had never happened before.

"Nothing's going on," Nina insisted.

"What date last weekend? You said you were just out with Melanie. Nina, you and I have never had secrets between us . . ."

"Okay, okay," she said, tossing her head back wearily. Her mother acted like Nina had committed a capital crime by letting down those who loved her the most. She didn't see what she had done wrong.

"Mom, look, I'm sorry I didn't totally level with you. I did meet a new boy, but it's no big deal."

Her mother looked as if she didn't agree.

"When you were my age," Nina said, "didn't you do something like this? Didn't you want to date different boys besides Dad? To feel free?"

Her mother thought a moment, as if trying to remember. Maybe she didn't want to remember, thought Nina. In the McKenzie home the past was as dead as the dinosaurs. Her parents' attitude was that because the past was impossible to change, it was pointless to discuss, even when Nina prodded.

"I know Melanie put you up to dating this boy," her mother said. "She's been a bad influence. I know that."

Nina rolled her eyes. "Maybe in the beginning, but I can think for myself, Mom."

"I know you can," and she gave Nina an understanding hug. Nina relaxed a little. She and her mom were close. She usually trusted her mom's judgment and perspective, and relied on her for advice. Being an only child, she felt her mother to be also her friend. At least she had in the past. But in the last few months, Nina realized, they'd had few intimate talks. She already knew how her parents felt about most issues. She realized she was starting to think and feel differently. Maybe she should have warned them that she was changing, but it was difficult to rock a boat that had been sailing for so long on smooth seas.

But now it was time. She had no choice.

"So there is someone." Her mother sat across from Nina at the table. "Poor Billy. Well, tell me about this boy."

"His name's Cliff. I like him a lot. You'd like him, too. Honest."

"What do you know about him?"

"Not much. His father was killed in Vietnam. He wants to be an officer. He's very mature, and different. I haven't met anyone like him."

"And he likes you?"

"Yes. I hope so anyway," she corrected herself, remembering her visit.

"Nina, I really don't think you should be seeing him anymore. You're lucky to have someone like Billy. Don't throw that away over nothing."

She shot up in her chair. "How do you know it's nothing?"

"Being in basic training means he'll be transferred to another fort soon. You can hardly expect to get to know him."

"Mom, I think the issue here is for me to be able to choose whomever I want to see, not whether there'll be a long-term relationship with someone I just met."

"Nina, you're being impulsive. It isn't like you."

"What do you mean, 'it isn't like me'? It *is* me." Her mother got a sharp look.

"Don't you think you owe Billy something?"

"I know I do, but what about me?" Frustrated, she marched into the living room and told Billy she had to talk to him. He followed uneasily to her room and closed the door.

"I really like you, Billy, you know that," she began, feeling the butterflies. "So this isn't easy for me to say . . ."

Billy dropped onto the bed, forking his fingers through his hair. "What's that supposed to mean?"

"I want to break up, at least for a while."

Billy looked stunned. Part of Nina couldn't believe what she'd said. She was used to pleasing people, not disappointing them.

"You're crazy," he scoffed. "We've been going together for two years. We're going to get married."

"Maybe two years is long enough."

"Nina, come on," he reasoned, still not believing her. He reached for her hand but she pulled back.

"Billy, I need a change."

"A change? From what?" he demanded. "For what?"

"A change in my life. I don't know exactly what I want to do, but I do know that I'm not happy with my plans. Going to Davis, marrying you, staying in Castroville . . . I feel that I'm missing out. I need something else, something more."

"I don't get it."

"It's how I feel."

She knew she'd hurt him.

"Why are you doing this to me?" he said.

"I'm not doing anything to you, Billy, not on purpose. I'm doing something *for* me."

"Haven't I been good to you?" he insisted. Sweat beaded on his forehead. "I love you."

"I know. I feel awful, but . . ."

"You're not yourself. You're infatuated with a soldier boy, that's it," he said angrily.

Maybe, thought Nina, but she couldn't be sure of what would happen between Cliff and her. The truth was she was throwing away her future and there was no safety net to fall into.

"You've got the whole world at your fingertips, including me," Billy said, "and you act like it's not good enough for you. You want more, better. You're spoiled—"

"That's not true!"

"What about me?" he charged. "Where's my future? Where's next week? We were supposed to go to the senior prom. Did you forget that? Do you care if the whole school laughs at me?"

"I'm really sorry. I know this isn't pleasant for you. It isn't for me either. But that's the way life is sometimes. It's not my fault."

"Well, I've got news for you, babe," he said, the anger shining through his voice. "You think I'm not good enough for you? Maybe you're not good enough for me. You lied to me. You went out with some guy behind my back—"

"Billy, I'm being honest now. Isn't that enough? I never meant to hurt you."

"You know," he snapped, jumping up, "you're going to be sorry you ever did this."

She couldn't believe it was sweet, accommodating Billy talking. He was so angry. He was trying to hurt her. Maybe he had a right to be upset, but couldn't he see her side of it? "Billy," she called, wanting to say goodbye, but he slammed the door and stormed out of the house.

Miserable, Nina dropped onto her bed. Everything felt out of control. She remembered telling Cliff about taking risks and facing the consequences, but she'd badly underestimated the consequences of her own acts. She picked up the phone and called Melanie. The phone rang a dozen times before she hung up in disgust. On instinct she called a hasty "I'll be back soon" to her parents and darted over to the record store. Melanie was in the demonstration booth, tapping her foot to a record.

"What's the matter?" Melanie said, startled, as she poked her head out. "You look like someone ran over your dog."

"I don't have a dog. It's you I want to run over," Nina blurted out.

"Hey, what's wrong with you?"

"It's your fault!"

Melanie looked distressed. "What's my fault?"

"I don't think Billy ever wants to see me again. He just walked out on me . . ."

"Isn't that what you wanted?"

"Maybe. I'm not sure. It's the way it all happened . . . He was so angry . . ."

"Calm down," Melanie said.

"And Cliff doesn't want to see me either."

"What?"

"I didn't tell you all that happened at the fort. He doesn't want to see me at all, I think."

Melanie looked sympathetic. "I'm sorry."

"Is that all you can say? Maybe my mother was right. You put me up to this. Take a chance, you said. You have to rebel once in a while. Life's an adventure, right?"

"Right," Melanie echoed, her voice trailing off as she studied her frustrated friend.

"Well, everything's ruined for me. My life's been turned upside down. I don't have Billy *or* Cliff. My parents think I've betrayed them. Thanks a lot, Melanie."

"Listen, don't get mad at me," Melanie shot back. "All I did was make suggestions. I made you ask yourself some questions. But I can't take responsibility for what happened. Your choices were your own. You haven't listened to me for months. Now you make a change. Fine. They're your decisions."

"No one said they weren't," Nina fumed. "I'm just sorry I listened to you in the first place. You never really cared about me—you were jealous of my having a boyfriend."

"That's not true!" Melanie shouted. "You're my best friend—"

"Some friend *you* are. You weren't even home when I called you. I had to find you in a record store. You're not making me feel any better."

Nina spun around, still furious. Melanie called after her but Nina's head didn't turn. That night she refused to come out of her room for dinner or talk to her parents. Peering into her mirror she thought she was looking at the world's biggest fool. But after a hot bath and lying in bed, she calmed down, trying to put events into focus. It had been a brutal day, but what had she expected? She had found the courage to make changes in her life. She knew logically that transitions never went smoothly. It had been ridiculous to bark at Melanie and blame her. Nina was as embarrassed as she was sorry for her outburst. She would have to apologize tomorrow.

For a moment she tried to imagine that the encounter with Billy had never taken place, that she could rewind the clock. But it was a pointless fantasy. What was done was done, and she sighed with relief that the fireworks were over. From here on things had to get better, didn't they? But there was no one to reassure her, and the silence of the night wouldn't allow an easy sleep. It was not that she wanted Cliff to replace Billy, but she wanted to be reassured it would all work out.

12

"A-tennn-hut!"

Boots clicked together slowly and bodies stood less than ramrod straight. As the sky faded into evening, the faces of the third platoon were portraits of exhaustion. Even Bradshaw, pacing restlessly in front of the formation, for once looked tired. But then a twenty-five-mile march in the rain would exhaust anyone. Cliff focused on the sergeant, wondering why he wouldn't let everyone just fall out to the barracks. All Cliff wanted was to collapse on his bed.

"We have a little problem, gentlemen," Bradshaw proclaimed as he continued his pacing. The empty, dirt-streaked faces stared back in a trance. "I was hoping one of you fine young men could help me solve it."

From his pocket he pulled what looked to Cliff like a credit card. "Two days ago, on Sunday, we had an unauthorized visitor to Charlie Company . . ."

Cliff looked again at the card in Bradshaw's hand.

It wasn't a credit card. It was a driver's license. The sergeant held it up to the fading light and scrutinized the photograph.

"I don't remember seeing this young lady here, but she must have been. Lost her license on the company street. Name's Melanie Connors." Bradshaw lifted his glance to the formation and showed off the miniature photo. "Anyone know a Melanie Connors?"

A suspicious Bradshaw had probably filched it from her purse, thought Cliff. He could see B.J. stiffen in the row in front of him.

"It's a mystery to me, scrotum heads, how this young lady got into our company. Only immediate family are allowed to visit. We don't have any trainee named Connors—do we?"

Trainees glanced at one another in tired confusion.

"I mean, Melanie Connors isn't someone's girlfriend, is she?" Bradshaw tacked down the front row until he stopped at B.J. Cliff knew it was all over. "Gibbons, your wife came to visit. But according to my records, you aren't married . . ."

"Yes, Sergeant," he said uneasily.

"Yes, Sergeant, what?"

"She was my girlfriend. It was my idea. I'm responsible." Unflinching, B.J. looked Bradshaw in the eye. He knew he would land back in the lion's den for this, but even if he didn't confess, Bradshaw would still punish him.

"What did you say, Gibbons?"

"I'm responsible."

"For what?"

Come on, B.J. thought, impatient in his fatigue, what was the point? Did Bradshaw want him to bleed in atonement? "For bringing the girls to Charlie Company, Sergeant."

"Girls?" Bradshaw inquired.

"It was my fault," B.J. repeated. He felt the sweat glide down his ribs. He wondered what his punishment would be.

"What girls? There was another girl?"

"Yes, Sergeant. Tall, blonde, good-looking . . ." B.J. stopped himself, but too late. He felt incredibly stupid.

"Tall, blonde, and good-looking," Bradshaw picked up. "Sure, I remember her. Your sister. Now what would she be coming along for? You don't have two girlfriends, do you, Maggot Gibbons?"

Bradshaw drifted over to Cliff. As tired as B.J. felt, he looked effervescent compared to his friend. Cliff's eyes were slits of exhaustion.

"Yes, Sergeant," B.J. called out loudly, "I do have two girlfriends. I've got five or six. I'm a real ladies' man, Sergeant."

"Sure, Gibbons." His eyes bored straight ahead into Cliff.

"You're wrong, Sergeant," B.J. shouted again. He wouldn't let this happen. He owed Cliff too much. "I'm the one who broke regulations. I'm your man."

"You're innocent, Gibbons."

"That's ridiculous. I organized the whole thing. Ask anyone. Next Sunday I'm bringing in half a dozen girls. . . ."

But Bradshaw had tuned out. His eyes riveted on Cliff with a hatred that made B.J. tremble. "You brought the girls in, isn't that right, Private Weigel?"

Cliff said nothing.

"Didn't you, troublemaker Weigel?"

Cliff didn't budge.

Bradshaw's finger poked him in the shoulder. "What was that, boy?"

"Yes." The voice was a raspy whisper.

"CAN'T HEAR YOU!"

"YES, SERGEANT, I BROUGHT THE GIRLS IN!"

B.J. was outraged. Cliff had confessed for the same reason he had, because he'd already been judged guilty.

"I could bust your tail for this, Weigel." The sergeant jutted his chin out. "I just don't want to yet. I'm not going to wash you out until the last second—I'd miss your sweet face too much." He gazed over at the low-crawl field, half-bathed in the evening shadows. A red ant colony the size of a small mountain sat in the middle. "Take off your clothes, Weigel."

Cliff stared back uncertainly.

"You heard."

When he didn't respond, Bradshaw slapped him across the face. Cliff peeled off his shirt. Down to his underwear, the sergeant marched him over to the ant colony.

On Bradshaw's orders, the rest of the platoon followed. B.J. felt sick.

"On your back, Weigel," Bradshaw commanded. Everyone watched the ants crisscrossing their mountain.

Enough, thought B.J., his indignation still building. Cliff was strong, but not that strong. He wasn't going to survive this. He wasn't going to graduate from basic training. Not unless someone helped him. With a courage he didn't have time to think about, B.J. flew at Bradshaw, aiming for his middle. The sergeant half-turned in defense, as if he'd seen B.J. out of a corner of his eye, but the trainee was already on him, fists thrashing down, an engine of fury.

Cliff watched as the sky darkened and the moon gained in luminosity. Lying spread-eagled, the ants traversed his body like an invading army, marching in columns up to his chin, reconnoitering his arms. His skin was sensitive to each whisper of feet, and the bites, when they came, were like sharp pinpricks that burned long afterward. He sensed that Bradshaw was watching from the NCO barracks, waiting for Cliff to panic, or at least to brush the ants from his face. Cliff did nothing. He would die, he promised himself, before asking Bradshaw for a sip of water.

His thoughts jumped to B.J. Everything had happened so quickly. Cliff had seen the raw anger in his friend's face, but B.J. was no match for Bradshaw, and once the sergeant had recovered from the surprise he'd pinned him down easily. Other sergeants had hustled over and hurried B.J. away—Cliff could only wonder to where.

The air grew cooler, but he realized his body was burning up. *You can't beat the Army, or this sergeant. It's against the rules. Like someone trying to steal first base . . .*

Bradshaw's words were etched into his mind and he'd begun to believe them. He knew the sergeant would keep him here all night. By morning he probably wouldn't even be able to stand. Maybe he wasn't the iron man he thought he was. Maybe this war with Bradshaw wasn't worth fighting after all. Even if he survived the ants, there was still two weeks before graduation, more of Bradshaw's torturous hoops to jump through.

Go on, give up, he thought.

Instead, he resisted the pain and drifted off to an uneasy sleep.

Something pulled his big toe. Cliff jerked his head up. The sky, except for a forlorn moon, was still black and empty. He was startled to look into Bradshaw's face. His leer lacked focus, and his hand cupped a can of beer.

"Get your butt out of here, Weigel," he said almost good-naturedly. "Go get some sleep."

He was startled by the reprieve. He struggled up, stiff and weak. "Where's B.J.?"

"Don't worry about your pal. Go back to the barracks."

"Where's B.J.?" Cliff repeated.

But Bradshaw was too drunk to answer. Instead he came over and looped an arm around Cliff, as if they were buddies. Cliff threw it off in disgust.

"Com'ere, Weigel," he called.

Cliff kept his distance.

". . . wanna show you something, boy." He coaxed a dog-eared colored photo from his pocket. The girl looked a little like Nina, but her hair wasn't quite so blonde nor her eyes as intelligent. "Name's Laurie," Bradshaw allowed in the silence. "She used to be my girl . . ."

Cliff started to turn away.

"Laurie thought she was too good for me," the sergeant said. "Queen of the planet. Dumped all over my head for some other guy. What do you think of that?"

Cliff was already dragging himself toward the barracks. Bradshaw demanded that he come back, a shrill, puny cry that broke the stillness of the night. Cliff ignored him and hobbled into the barracks.

13

Cliff half-expected Bradshaw to follow. Instead of footsteps he heard a symphony of exhausted breathing on the bay. He hovered by B.J.'s bunk but the covers had never been pulled back. Checking the latrine he got lucky. Crumpled at the bottom of a shower stall, B.J. looked half dead. Cold water sprayed down on a face that had been beaten raw. One whole side was swollen and blue. An eye was locked shut.

"What happened?" Cliff asked when B.J. looked up.

"What do you think?" he whispered hoarsely.

"Tell me."

"Bradshaw said he could stick me in the stockade for assaulting a noncommissioned officer. But he didn't want to do that . . . he said he'd let me off easy . . . The other sergeants left the room."

Cliff glanced sharply in the direction of the NCO barracks.

"Don't even think it," B.J. warned. "It's not worth it."

"We know that creep's not fit for the Army," Cliff said. "The Army should know it, too."

"How are you going to do that?"

"I don't know. I'd love to figure out a way. Come on, let me help you up."

B.J. rose in pain. "You know, I don't care about revenge," he said. "All I think about is graduation. Two weeks seems like an eternity."

"We'll make it, I give you my word," Cliff swore. "After what happened tonight, nothing's going to stop me."

"I really don't understand you," B.J. said. "I know you want to be an officer, but so do a lot of people. You're obsessed."

With pride Cliff told B.J. all about his father, and why he was in the Army.

"But Vietnam?" B.J. said. "That was so long ago. How old were you when he was killed?" B.J. was pleased to hear something personal from Cliff.

"I was too young to remember him, if that's what you mean."

"What I mean is, he wouldn't want you to kill yourself over this. He was probably an understanding guy. You've created an image of perfection."

"To me he's flesh and blood. My mother told me all about him. He was a great soldier. He'll always be alive to me. Not just for what he stood for, but for what I think he wanted me to be."

B.J. nodded, trying to understand.

"He's an ideal," Cliff explained. "Something that

116

nobody can tear down. I won't let anybody tear him down. His memory is all I have. It's special to me."

B.J. saw the fierce love in Cliff's face. It shone through his exhaustion, his hatred for Bradshaw, and it made B.J. envious. Why couldn't he have some ideal like that?

When Cliff slipped off to bed, B.J. stared blankly out a moon-silvered window. He was a prisoner in the Army, he thought, no rights, no freedom, no hope. All he had to keep him going was what was inside him. He knew he was no Cliff, but maybe he had some resources to sustain him. Going after Bradshaw tonight had showed some courage finally. And Melanie, he had her, too, didn't he? With an effort B.J. pulled on some clothes and walked out of the barracks. There wasn't a muscle that didn't ache or burn. He took a secondary road to the PX, hiding from the few oncoming headlights, and reached a bank of pay phones silhouetted by a floodlight.

Melanie's phone rang ten times. B.J. refused to hang up. Was he crazy to call at two in the morning? What if Melanie's mother answered?

"Hello," came a groggy but sweet voice.

B.J.'s chest heaved in relief. "Hi," he said. "It's me."

"B.J.?"

"How are you?"

"Do you know what time it is? Are you all right?"

"This is the only time I can get to a phone."

"What's the matter, you sound down . . ."

"I'm really happy to be talking to you," was all he wanted to say.

"I don't understand."

"What's there to understand?" he asked. "I miss you. I love you. I wanted to hear your voice."

"I love you, too," she said. "And I'm coming to see you again—"

"No," he interrupted, "you can't do that."

"Why not?"

"You just can't. Don't worry, somehow I'll see you when basic is over."

"B.J., what's going on?" she demanded. "Level with me . . ."

He didn't want to tell her. There was no point in making more waves. "Bradshaw knows about you and Nina. He got hold of your driver's license somehow. You can't come back."

"He found out?" she said, worried. "What did he do?"

"Nothing," he managed.

"You're sure?"

"He just blew his top."

"B.J., you don't sound right. Are you sure you're okay?"

"Sure." Headlights suddenly exploded off the glass booth, and he turned with a start. "Melanie, I've got to run. I love you—"

"Don't hang up. I want to see you. I don't want to wait till after basic . . ."

"No," he said again and clicked down the receiver. He darted out of the phone booth and behind the PX before the MP's jeep could catch up with him. He waited for footsteps, got nervous, and ran anyway, panting all the way to the barracks.

Safe, he thought, and almost laughed. Safe in prison.

He was in too much pain to sleep. Sitting up he noticed that someone had left his day's mail. Good old Bobby Douglas. He'd written back.

Dear Defender of Our Country,

Hello again from Goof-Off High! Nothing terribly new to report except that I finally got a date with Sally Barnes—the girl of my dreams. I asked if she would come to our last basketball game and she said she would. My strategy was to score a lot of points for the old team and in so doing score a few with Sally, too. In the first quarter I took an elbow in the eye and was forced to sit out the game. I mean, I couldn't believe my luck. I figured Sally wouldn't be too impressed but after the game she gave me a big kiss—like I was some kind of hero! And now we're going out. You never know what girls are thinking, do you? Hey, pal, sure didn't know what to make of your last letter. A rat hunt under the barracks? Is this something my friendly local recruiter can tell me about? To be perfectly honest, B.J., I've given up any thoughts about enlisting. Reading between the lines of your letters has given me an uneasy feeling. I can't tell if you're really happy with the Army or not. Hey, better run—graduation rehearsal. Nine more days and I'm a free man. Then what? Haha.

Bobby

B.J. read the letter again. *Then what?* Bobby, you fool, he thought. If you had to ask, you'd never know. Being free—B.J. imagined a happy scene: to be out, to be with Melanie . . . Why be a prisoner in the Army anyway? He didn't have the burning compulsion or natural ability of a Cliff. Bradshaw wanted to wash him out—why not go out with the tide? He'd failed before. What was one more failure now? B.J.'s mind filled with his fantasies the rest of the night.

But in the morning, when reveille sounded, he showered and dressed before the rest of the platoon was up. Ignoring his pain, he managed to be the first in formation, and felt proud that Bradshaw hadn't beaten him down.

14

A distracted Nina huddled with her friends, waiting for the first-period bell. She kept one eye out for Melanie. Before breakfast Melanie had phoned with the news that B.J. had called late last night, and that something was up. Nina didn't know whether this was typical Melanie melodrama or something genuine, but worried about Cliff, she wanted to know more.

After facing Billy, Nina had finally confronted her mother and father. Not only was she relieved to have broken up with Billy, she admitted to them, but she was having doubts about her whole future. There was more to life, maybe, than going to college, getting married and having children. What about taking a year off and traveling? Going to New York and just being on her own? Everyone around her was so conservative that it felt confining. Nina felt that her parents looked at her as if she was no longer their daughter. They blamed Melanie, but when Nina de-

fended her friend they picked on Cliff. She was forbid
den to go back to Fort Ord. Nina knew no one was t
blame. People had a right to change. She refused t
feel guilty, and she resented her parents for not un
derstanding.

"Why isn't Billy right for you anymore?" he
mother asked again and again. "Why?"

"Because he's not what I want," Nina answered.

"Then what do you want?"

"I'm not sure. I'll tell you when I find out."

Beneath her bold statements Nina worried. What i
she didn't find a boyfriend as nice as Billy? What i
she chose the wrong college, or the wrong career, and
ended up wasting her life? Melanie kept reminding
her how much potential she had, that she was free t
use it as she pleased, but Nina wasn't accustomed t
freedom. Her life had always been structured by goals
and expectations. She was so used to the satisfactior
that came with success that she wondered if she could
live differently.

Nina picked her head up as two senior girls strolled
by, trading whispers. People were talking about her
and Billy breaking up. Was it spring fever on Nina's
part? Had she flipped? Nina told herself she didn't
care about the gossip but down deep it bothered her
She was used to fame, not notoriety. Overnight her
fishbowl life had begun to be scrutinized in ways that
ripped at her image. The really catty people were actually suggesting that she had never had her act together. It made her furious.

"There you are," Nina exclaimed when she finally
spotted Melanie.

122

Nina's other friends shot Melanie a distrustful glance as she motioned Nina away.

"So what's the big news?" Nina demanded.

"I think B.J.'s in trouble."

"How do you know?"

"Why would he call me up in the middle of the night? Just to say hello?"

"Maybe."

"That's what *he* said. I don't buy it. Remember I told you I was missing my driver's license? Bradshaw ended up with it. That's all B.J. would tell me, and that we couldn't go back to the fort. I think Bradshaw's making him miserable."

"What did B.J. say about Cliff?"

"Nothing. Just the same air of mystery. I'm going to find out what's happening . . ."

"How?"

"I'll sneak back into the fort. I'm going to save B.J.," she vowed.

The first-period warning bell blared across the yard. Nina wanted to know more, wondering if she shouldn't join Melanie, but they had to scamper in opposite directions. Nina felt for Cliff. Not only had she possibly screwed up her own life, she'd hurt his, too. She wanted to see him again, even if he might not want to see her.

Nina hesitated as she approached the administration building. Billy was lingering on the steps, looking more handsome than ever. A contented twinkle was in his eyes. A new man. What right did he have to look happy when she was feeling so down? Maybe she'd missed Billy more than she'd realized. For a moment she wished they were together again. That she was rejecting marriage didn't mean they couldn't date. She could see Billy *and* Cliff, couldn't she?

Nina was moving toward her former boyfriend with a penitent smile when something caught her eye. Another girl strolled up from behind and playfully cupped her hands over Billy's eyes. "Guess who?" the girl flirted. Billy laughed as their hands joined. Nina overheard only one sentence. Something about the senior prom.

She felt sick to her stomach as she tried to accept what was happening. When Billy caught her looking at him, she pretended to be cheerful and hurried off to class.

15

Bradshaw shielded his eyes from the late afternoon sun and directed the platoon into a horseshoe formation around Cliff. Everyone was dirty and exhausted. The sergeant had already brought out a chair and small table, along with an umbrella, and with a poker face he now set two candles in the middle. Cliff was ordered to sit in the shaded chair as a KP brought out a charcoal-broiled steak decked with mushrooms.

"Go ahead, Private Weigel, eat up," Bradshaw said almost cordially. Cliff picked up his fork and knife and hesitantly cut off a bite.

Was this a joke? Cliff felt eyes poring over him, mouths watering. Lunch had been hours ago, a couple of cans of C rations during the day march, and breakfast no one could remember. Taking off his hat, Bradshaw made a lazy loop around the formation. The boyish face showed mock exasperation.

"Worms, I observed a very unfortunate thing today," he said. "I saw some trainees talking to Private Weigel on the march. Talking to the enemy. That was against my orders . . ."

Cliff put down his fork, waiting for what would come next. The sergeant had ordered a code of silence all week for Cliff; he couldn't talk to anyone, and no one could talk to him. Intimidated, everyone had stayed clear except for B.J. He and Cliff met in the latrine when the barracks lights went off, and sometimes they got to talk after lunch, before the afternoon formation. In the beginning the punishment hadn't fazed Cliff, but after a few days he felt like climbing the walls. Everybody acted as if he was contaminated. The only thing he looked forward to all day was hearing B.J.'s voice. But on the march today he hadn't made contact with anyone; it would have been too dangerous. Bradshaw was jerking him around again.

"Naturally, worms, those who broke the code will have to be punished. My problem is I can't be certain who the offenders were. I saw everything from a distance. It could have been anyone. That means I'll have to punish everybody."

Groans of anger and dismay.

"Isn't that fair, worms?"

Silence.

"ISN'T THAT FAIR?"

"Yes, Sergeant!"

"THEN GET ON YOUR BACKS BEFORE I RUN YOU ALL UP HEARTBREAK HILL!"

Reference to the fort's steep and dusty hill that trainees had to run up and down regularly brought Cliff more hostile glances. He was being blamed for this. Pushing his steak away, he watched as everyone dropped to the asphalt and assumed the dying-cockroach position. Cliff was more than familiar with the torture. Bradshaw put him through it a dozen times a week. Arms and legs were extended and held rigidly in the air. Only your butt was allowed to touch the ground. After a couple of minutes the trainees' moaning grew louder and limbs became wavering antennae. One by one the cockroaches collapsed and Bradshaw ordered them to flip over on their stomachs. The sergeant marched up to B.J.

"Hungry, cockroach Gibbons?"

"Yes, Sergeant."

"How hungry?"

"Very hungry."

"Then eat."

Cliff saw the mix of confusion and frustration on B.J.'s face.

"Cockroaches eat dirt, didn't you know that, Gibbons?"

Reluctantly, B.J.'s tongue licked the asphalt.

Bradshaw made everyone else do the same.

"You poor cockroaches have to eat dirt while Private Weigel enjoys steak," Bradshaw observed. "Does that seem fair?"

Cliff looked out on a sea of angry faces. He knew that most trainees were sympathetic to what he'd been through, but under the hot sun, on empty stomachs, sucking asphalt, it was different.

"I don't like it, Sergeant," one trainee spoke up. He was heavyset with a neck as thick as a tree stump. He rose and glared at Cliff.

"You don't like it?" Bradshaw aped in pretend astonishment. "You don't *like* it? Well, what are you going to do *do* about it?"

Like a sprinter out of the blocks, the boy bulled into the table, sending it flying and Cliff along with it.

B.J. watched, disbelieving, as the boy's fists pummeled Cliff. He wouldn't fight back, as usual, but this time he was getting creamed. Hoarse, half-crazed cheers rose from the platoon until Bradshaw finally intervened. Cliff rose shakily, his hair matted with blood, his face swollen as badly as B.J.'s had been.

"Everyone hates you, boy," Bradshaw said to Cliff. "The whole company hates you. The United States Army hates you. Nobody thinks you're a soldier. We think you're a pussycat. Can't even defend yourself boy . . ."

B.J. glared at Bradshaw. As the sergeant ordered Cliff out on all-night guard duty, B.J. walked up, in plain view of everyone, and gave his friend a pat on the shoulder. Bradshaw saw, but B.J. didn't care. In the barracks he washed the dirt out of his mouth and collapsed on his bunk, trying to calm himself. In the day's mail, he found a letter from his mother telling him the house had been repainted. Another was from a former girlfriend doing well in college. Nothing from Bobby. B.J. focused on the last envelope. The perfume was Melanie's. His spirits picked up as he opened it quickly.

> Dearest B.J.,
>
> You should get this letter by Friday. If so, tonight's the night! Tell your duty officer that you're sick and we'll meet at the battalion infirmary around 10:00 P.M. It's all legit accord-

ing to the regulations book. I miss you so much, B.J. Put a smile on your handsome face. I have good news!

With all my love,
M.

B.J. tore up the letter and flushed the scraps down the toilet. After a shower he put on fresh fatigues while his mind spun crazily. Good news? What did she mean? All he wanted was to be with Melanie again. But how would he get to the infirmary? An appendicitis attack sounded like a winner. The only problem was he knew that Bradshaw was the duty NCO tonight. B.J. considered just sneaking off and taking his chances, but what if someone caught him by the infirmary? Better to kick and scream in mock pain and get the sergeant's official permission.

All through dinner he looked at his watch. Afterward as trainees milled toward the barracks, he spotted Bradshaw near the NCO quarters, tossing a football with his sergeant buddies. He did that a lot. Tonight he had both his high school jersey and helmet on. He took a lot of pride in the uniform, and in the glory days of high school, B.J. guessed, thinking of his own past. In the barracks, when everyone was asleep, B.J. levered himself off the spongy mattress and headed toward company headquarters. From other barracks came the illicit glow of cigarettes. A lone window in headquarters cast a slanted, squarish light on the street. B.J. knocked on the door. When there was no answer he pushed his head in.

"Sergeant?" he called in a voice he didn't recognize. His hand snaked to his appendix. "Sergeant Bradshaw?"

An interior door was open. A harsh, gray light spilled out in lines on the floor. B.J. listened curiously, almost having forgotten what a television was. Bradshaw's head was slumped on the desk. Rough snoring interrupted the movie he'd been watching.

At the sergeant's elbow was a *National Geographic* with slips of wilted paper hanging from the top. B.J. knew he was crazy as he walked over and picked up the magazine. But he felt a curious power over the sleeping sergeant, safe from his wrath for the moment, and able, if he wanted, to finally hurt Bradshaw. He wasn't that brave. Still, he was brave enough to flip to the magazine's marked pages, daring Bradshaw to wake. Lush photos of a vineyard in France, beaches in Sri Lanka, Buddhist temples in Burma. Were these destinations the sergeant's dreams? Cliff had told B.J. about Bradshaw's admission of a broken love affair, and maybe that was why he'd enlisted. And a cook had confided that Bradshaw had once applied for Officer Candidate School, only to be turned down. So here he was, stuck in the Army as a drill instructor, jealous of anyone going to OCS. The best times of his life were already behind him.

Putting the magazine down, B.J. toyed with the idea of waking the sergeant for his infirmary pass, but what if he were angry at the intrusion? Smarter now just to sneak off.

Even from a distance, B.J. recognized the convertible parked a safe distance from the shoebox of an infirmary. Melanie jumped out and rushed into his arms. He gave her a long kiss before he stepped back in surprise. She looked terrific. He noticed she'd cut her hair short, and her gold loop earrings gave her an elegant look. She no longer looked like a high school senior.

"I knew you'd make it," she said, relieved, as they ducked back into the car.

"I've missed you. Really missed you," B.J. confessed.

"Me, too." She kissed him again before pulling back abruptly and peering at his cheek. B.J. knew bruises from Bradshaw's beating were still visible.

"What happened?" she demanded.

He shrugged. "I fell down."

"Look me in the eye . . ."

"Hey, come on."

"Tell me the truth!"

B.J. forgot his pride. How could he deceive Melanie if he really loved her? "Okay. The sergeant treated me like a punching bag."

"Why? You're trying hard, aren't you?"

"The man isn't human."

"What are you going to do?"

B.J. shook his head in frustration. "Sometimes I feel like walking away from the Army. I can't see butting my head against this wall forever. Maybe my niche isn't here. I know it would be one more failure, but if I could get out, be free again, things might be different."

"I can help you," she said suddenly. B.J. looked at her. "That's my good news."

"What good news?"

Melanie glanced nervously at B.J. Was she crazy to suggest this? What if B.J. thought so? Nina would say she was headstrong, but that was her nature, and this was what she wanted. In another ten days she'd be eighteen, ready to graduate, an adult. She could do whatever she wanted. From her purse she pulled a thick Army manual and thumbed to the middle. "You know, I've read this whole manual cover to cover," she announced. "I've practically memorized portions. I don't even have to read them to you, I could recite them. I bet I could write an Army manual myself . . ."

B.J. wondered why she was so nervous.

"Did you know," she said, "that if you're needed by a civilian employer for something crucial, like a defense industry job, you can ask for a discharge? If your parents die or get sick and you have to support a younger sibling, it's the same thing. Or you contract a debilitating illness while in the service . . . Or . . ." She hesitated. "Or you get married, and your wife needs you to support her."

B.J. looked at Melanie as the silence wrapped them. It took him a moment to comprehend. "We can get married," she said for him anyway. "Of course, there's more to it than that, the wife has to have special needs, but we can fake that, I know we can. We can do anything we want, can't we, B.J.?" She stopped herself, knowing she was rambling.

"You want us to get married?" B.J. said, still shocked.

"It's not such a crazy idea. We're in love. I adore you. Don't you feel that way about me?"

"It's not my emotions," he said. "It's just that marriage is a big step, a permanent step. It's something to think about."

"I have thought about it. We'll be happy together.

And you want your freedom. We both want that. We won't need much money . . . we can get rich later . . ."

B.J. shook his head.

"You're afraid," she said.

"That's not it."

"Then you don't really love me."

"I do love you."

"Then what? Do you want more time to know me?" she asked.

"Maybe," he admitted. He was trying to be honest, but his answers were disappointing her. When he searched Melanie's face all he saw was anxiety. Beneath her impulsiveness and romantic spirit she was insecure, even fragile, he realized, and he didn't want to hurt her. What else could he say? The idea of marriage had been dropped on him like a stick of dynamite, and he didn't know how to react. He didn't know his own emotions. And part of him, his pride, still wanted to gut it out in the Army. In spite of Bradshaw, he wanted to prove he could succeed at something.

A lone tear rolled down Melanie's cheek. B.J. took her in his arms. "Don't worry," he said. "This will work out. We'll work it out together."

She snuggled closer, trembling as her breathing grew more rapid. He wanted to protect her, so she would never get hurt, but he wasn't sure how. "I've got to get back before I'm missed," he said. After a minute they kissed goodbye. B.J. promised to sneak to a phone tomorrow night. Drifting into the damp night, he wondered what he would tell her.

16

The fog rolled off the ocean in thick clouds, blanketing the highway as Melanie drove unsteadily home. She had stopped her tears but her uneasy feelings wouldn't go away. Tonight she had gone out on a limb, further than she ever had, telling B.J. how much she loved him. Marriage was the ultimate commitment. But B.J. had reacted with a cold rationality that surprised and hurt her. Maybe he wasn't the fellow romantic she'd hoped. He acted as if he didn't want to be free, or as if marriage didn't mean freedom. Melanie first thought she'd gone too far, expected too much. Was B.J. instantly supposed to set a wedding date and plan their honeymoon?

Haunting her now was the thought that B.J. really wanted to tell her no. He just didn't have the guts. Or maybe, she hoped, he didn't know what he wanted.

Well, *she* knew, and she wasn't going to change her mind.

Melanie guided the car onto the highway shoulder

and kept the radio on. With the top down, the breeze wafted over her. Her perch looked over a turbulent ocean, but the way the fog gently wrapped around the moon, diffusing the light, she saw as hope. You had to have hope to live. She and B.J. would be married, she knew it. She would be happy and fulfilled, and in spite of his doubts now, so would B.J. The radio continued to sing to her. She dropped her head against the seat, dreaming.

When Melanie opened her eyes a pink line edged across the horizon like a fine brush stroke. The sun exploded off a distant corner of the ocean. She was startled to hear the hum of traffic. Her mother would have a cow that she'd been gone all night. Rubbing her eyes, Melanie flicked over the ignition key. The engine gave a faint whir and turned silent. Damn, she thought, she'd forgotten to turn off the radio. Resigned, she groped out of the car, raised the hood, and pushed her thumb out to traffic.

No handsome soldier came to her rescue. The man was middle-aged, overweight, balding, and hardly said a word to Melanie. He gave her a lift as far as the nearest gas station, where she waited two more hours before a tow truck could take her back to her car.

17

It was a cattle stampede.

The forty trainees of the Third Platoon, elbows jostling and lungs hungry for air, began the assault on Heartbreak Hill in a wavering mass. As the afternoon heat broke in shimmers over the wilderness of scrub and chaparral, heels kicked up coils of dust that hung lazily in the still air. Cliff's thoughts were focused on finishing. Three miles in under eighteen minutes. That was the test. He had done it a half dozen times, and he would do it again. Then his torment would be over. Eight weeks of basic done, forgotten. This morning Bradshaw had given everyone a final test on the rifle range, in bayonet drill, and on the obstacle course. Cliff had passed everything with ease, even while keeping a nervous eye on his sergeant. To his surprise there had been no tricks. Had Bradshaw finally given up, or was this the lull before the storm? Cliff didn't want to think about it. All that stood between him and graduation now was Heartbreak Hill.

He broke in front of the pack by taking long, easy strides, conserving his energy. B.J. wasn't too far back. He'd done well on the morning tests, too, landing in the top ten percent, which had surprised everyone. With all his ups and downs, B.J. was turning out to be officer material after all. The pounding of the herd grew more distant as Cliff picked up speed. Sweat glided down his ribs. The hill suddenly loomed before him, a signal that there was only one mile to go. He thought of the graduation ceremonies scheduled for Saturday. He could finally visualize himself in his dress greens, the gold Private First Class stripes on his shoulder. Tonight he would call his mother with the good news. He knew his father would have been especially proud.

Cliff glanced behind him, leery. But there was no Bradshaw, just the rest of his platoon. He sprinted the last quarter mile to the finish line. He saw the sergeant now, a stopwatch looped around his neck, and beside him the company clerk with a clipboard to record the times. Cliff stepped defiantly across the finish so there would be no doubt. He leaned over and caught his breath. The clerk ran up and told him he'd made the run under fifteen minutes, a company record.

Bradshaw swaggered up, waiting till Cliff met his eyes.

"Looks like you'll have to run the course again, boy," he said matter of factly.

Cliff wondered who he was talking to.

"You cheated, Private Weigel. Stepped out of bounds coming down the hill. Saw you clear as day."

Cliff bolted up. "I didn't step out," he said.

"Are you *arguing* with me?"

"I didn't step out—you know it!"

"I saw you, Weigel," Bradshaw announced coolly. "So did my clerk."

The young man glanced away. Cliff began to boil, his red face turning redder. "Look, I ran the three miles faster than anyone else—"

"Too bad, boy." Bradshaw's eyes were already pointing to the starting line. "A trainee in your shape shouldn't have any problems."

Furious, Cliff spat on the ground. He watched as the first wave of runners streamed down the hill to the finish—and *he* had to run the course all over? He reached for a canteen but Bradshaw grabbed it away. Cliff said nothing. He kept his anger inside as he broke from the starting line, using it to pump his adrenaline. His watch read exactly three. He would make it, he promised himself. But as his legs carried him over the hard ground they felt untrustworthy. His chest ached. The cumulative punishments of the last month were catching up.

When he reached the base of Heartbreak Hill his watch read three-ten. The cramping in his calves made him shorten his stride but he still thought he could make it. Only his dehydration really bothered him. He was weak. Reaching the peak he began the run home. He saw B.J. at the finish, shouting him on, defying Bradshaw's code of silence. Then the whole company began to cheer. Bradshaw did nothing. His face was inscrutable.

Cliff stumbled across the finish and collapsed in the dirt. B.J. led a final yell of triumph. The fire in Cliff's lungs seemed unquenchable, but he had finished, on time, and he would tolerate the pain.

"Son of a gun," Bradshaw lamented as he strolled over. Trainees kept a wary distance. "My stopwatch quit on me. A spring must have broken. I'm really sorry, Weigel—guess what?"

Cliff's whole body trembled. He was too tired to speak, to raise himself. He should have known. He would never graduate from basic. If he conquered Heartbreak Hill five times, Bradshaw would ask for six. He wiped the sweat from his eyes and tried to stand. Pain everywhere.

"Are you giving up, boy?" Bradshaw asked. A faint smile floated on his lips.

Cliff stared back defiantly.

"Say you're licked, Weigel. Tell me I've beaten you. Tell the whole platoon how I won our war."

"No," he said in a shaky voice.

"You fought well, maggot. You held up longer than anyone else who ever went against me. But now you're beaten. Face it."

"You haven't won anything," Cliff said with a forcefulness that surprised even himself.

Bradshaw looped his thumbs over his canteen belt. "You're too proud, boy. You've always been too proud. That's your weakness. I found it, and that's why I won."

"Proud, just like you."

"Right," Bradshaw acknowledged. "Except that I'm the sergeant, and you're the private."

Kiss my butt, thought Cliff.

139

"Tell everyone I won, worm."

With an effort Cliff pulled himself up. His arms felt like they'd fall off. "No way," he said.

"Admit I won," he announced for everyone to hear, "and I'll let you graduate from basic."

It was a tease, Cliff thought, another head game. He scrutinized the sergeant. In the benign silence Bradshaw repeated his offer. Cliff's glance swam to B.J., who nodded that he should accept. Did B.J. believe that the sergeant was on the level? In his combat with Bradshaw, maybe Cliff had lost perspective. The sergeant thought he'd won the war; this might be the amnesty.

"What's your answer, boy?"

Cliff's boot pawed at the ground. He remembered the promise he had made Nina in the mess hall, that silently he made to himself. He'd gut it out till graduation. To think of surrendering made him feel cowardly. Not just for reasons of pride, but because it would be saying that Bradshaw's games of punishment were okay, that they'd always be okay. Cliff could graduate, but what about the next trainee who became the platoon scapegoat?

"What are you going to do, Weigel?"

He looked the sergeant in the eye. "I'm going to run the course again."

Cliff caught B.J. grimacing. Bradshaw's face showed surprise, then anger, as if he thought his generosity was being mocked. It was the same reaction as when Cliff had chosen B.J. for the pass.

For the third time Cliff toed the starting line, waiting for Bradshaw to get a new stopwatch. The air felt like an oven. His fatigues were already drenched with sweat, but he pushed off cleanly, refusing to think of the sun or his thirst. After the first mile his legs turned rubbery. The landscape began to blur. With the hill looming before him he suddenly stopped, his lungs burning. Then, worried about time, he ran again. Halfway up, out of sight of the platoon and Bradshaw, he collapsed in the dirt. He was embarrassed that he couldn't stand. His stomach heaved.

This time, Cliff knew, he wasn't going to make it.

Something stirred behind him. A hand slipped under his arm and pulled Cliff to a sitting position. He looked up at B.J. as if he were an apparition. In B.J.'s hand was a canteen.

"Drink," ordered his friend.

Cliff took several gulps of water, and emptied the rest of the canteen on his head.

"What are you doing here?" Cliff breathed.

"I sneaked away from Bradshaw and the platoon."

"Get back before you're caught."

"I'll take my chances." B.J. helped Cliff up. "Do me a favor. You're half-dead. Even if you finish this run you won't make the next. Go back and tell Bradshaw you're sorry. I know that's hard, but it's the smart way, the only way."

"It's wrong."

"I'll tell you what's wrong," B.J. said. "Not finishing basic. Not becoming an officer. That's your dream."

The sweat glided down Cliff's face. He blinked out the sun.

"You can do it," B.J. said. "You can do anything you want to. Go back and tell him, and you'll wipe the man out of your life forever."

Cliff grabbed a breath. He really was tired of the fighting, he thought. B.J. was being a friend, a wise one, and Cliff knew he should take his advice. There would be other wars to fight and win.

"Okay," he said. "I'll go back."

A shadow dropped across his path before he could take a step. Bradshaw's face was bright with anger. B.J. froze. Cliff took a step forward.

"I can't finish the run, Sergeant," Cliff said after a moment. He expected Bradshaw to be appeased, even happy, but the glare stayed on his face. "It's all over," Cliff explained. "You won."

"Won what, maggot? You cheated. Your buddy just gave you water . . ."

Why all the doubletalk? Cliff wondered. Why did Bradshaw keep pushing? He was never satisfied. Did he think that Cliff's surrender had come too quickly, or that because B.J. had intervened, Cliff hadn't really been defeated?

"I'm taking back my offer," Bradshaw said. "You failed the run. You fail basic training."

Cliff stared at him.

"You're out of the Army forever. What do you think about that, Weigel?"

The outrage swept over Cliff.

"You don't deserve to graduate. You never did."

Cliff waited till his composure came back. "Sergeant, you're lower than a bastard."

"Getting pissed off, boy? You don't want to lose your cool, do you? Because I know you think you're cool. You've never lost your temper. You don't believe in fistfights. A matter of pride and principle, right? The perfect soldier boy . . ."

Cliff saw the game now. Kicking him out of the Army wasn't enough. Bradshaw was trying to bait him. That was how the sergeant would claim his final victory. Well, let him try, Cliff thought. He'd already surrendered to Bradshaw once—never again.

Bradshaw reached out and grabbed B.J. by the neck. Forcing the trainee to the ground, the sergeant sliced his boot into his rib cage. B.J. moaned. "Isn't the perfect soldier going to rescue his buddy?" Bradshaw demanded.

Cliff did nothing.

"Your friend's not helping you," Bradshaw hissed in B.J.'s ear. "What kind of friend is that?" When B.J. stayed silent, the sergeant tightened his grip. "What kind of friend? He's a sleazeball, Gibbons. Tell him he's a sleazeball—"

"Let go of him," said Cliff.

"What was that, boy?"

"Leave him alone."

"What if I don't?"

Cliff took a step forward.

"Are you threatening your sergeant, Weigel? Are you going to fight? That's what you've always wanted to do. You hate everything about me—isn't that right?"

"I'm not going to touch you."

"Chicken?"

No, thought Cliff, but he wouldn't give in.

Bradshaw let go of B.J. and kicked at a pebble. He was getting frustrated, Cliff saw. "I was reading your personnel file last night, Weigel," he spoke up. "Pretty impressive. High IQ. Good grades. All-state in football. Just like me. Did you know I was all-state, too?"

"I couldn't really care, Sergeant."

"You couldn't care? You think you're better than me, Weigel? Just because I couldn't get into OCS and you think you have?"

Walk away, Cliff told himself.

"Interesting stuff about your old man," Bradshaw suddenly threw in.

Cliff was startled.

"He won a lot of medals," the sergeant said. "Bronze Star, Silver Star, Purple Heart. Is that why you're in the Army? Are you going to win medals, too? You want to be a hero like him?"

"That's none of your business," Cliff said.

"Was he real proud like you, Weigel?"

The company clerk and a handful of trainees had drifted up, and now stood with B.J. "He was a great soldier," Cliff answered.

"He was a total phony. Half his medals were given out of pity because he got his face blown off. I know the colonel who recommended them."

"That's a lie."

"Did you know that the men he commanded hated him? I checked, boy."

"That's a lie!"

"He loved blood and guts. He was a weirdo."

"You're just talking about yourself, Sergeant!"

"Sure I am. I'd say your old man was a loser."

Cliff felt his temper building. He couldn't let Bradshaw get away with this, defame his father. Cliff's memories couldn't be destroyed.

"A first class yo-yo . . . some old man . . ."

"I'm warning you!" Cliff said. He pointed a finger at the sergeant.

144

"My, my, what do we have here? A trainee on the brink of losing control?"

"Shut your mouth! You don't have the right to even say my father's name!"

"You know something else about your father? He wished to hell he never had a kid—"

Cliff sprung toward his enemy and toppled him like a matchstick. B.J. wagged his head to stop Cliff, but he pounded the sergeant's face without mercy. Blood spurted from Bradshaw's nose, then his eyes sealed over. Cliff couldn't stop. Only when he felt the swarm of arms pulling him off did he feel the relief from getting out his hatred and realize what he had done.

18

After lunch period Nina and Melanie paraded into the auditorium with the rest of the student body. As the lights dimmed, the faculty assumed their places on stage and the principal stood behind the lectern with the solemnity of a minister. He waited for the din of conversation to recede.

"My last assembly," Melanie declared. "I'm all choked up. Which award do you think Mr. Humphrey will give me—best attitude, or most contributions to the school?"

"Least likely ever to come back to a class reunion," Nina quipped.

"That's right," Melanie affirmed, "they won't have this gadfly to kick around anymore."

Nina's eye wandered to Billy and his new girlfriend, Donna, several rows ahead. They were holding hands. Why did she feel so jealous? She'd broken up with Billy, not the other way around. Yet she couldn't put him out of her thoughts. Several imes she'd wanted to call him, or stop him in the schoolyard, but her pride wouldn't let her.

It wasn't Billy or Donna she was jealous of, she'd finally decided; it was the past, what Nina had lost. Most kids would die to have what she'd thrown away—practically engaged to the town's wealthiest boy, a secure future. What was also hard to accept was that she had no new plans. After being a success for so long she was suddenly afraid of encountering failure. Her parents had helped feed her doubts. After the initial shock at her rebellion, they'd changed tactics. Whatever Nina wanted to do, they said, was all right with them. The reverse psychology was pure deviousness.

The principal rapped his gavel to kill the last whispers, and pushed his weathered face toward the microphone. "Good afternoon. As you know, every year at this time it's my privilege to wish the senior class Godspeed as they embark on their futures. It's also my privilege to single out those outstanding individuals who have contributed to our school and its traditions . . ."

Nina slouched restlessly. Mr. Humphrey gave the same speech every year—she knew it by heart—but this time she was a senior and it was supposed to be meaningful. She listened as he named the outstanding athlete, science student, student body officer . . . One by one, the chosen few marched up to receive a warm handshake and robust applause.

"I've saved the best for the last," Mr. Humphrey announced. "It's my honor to present the award to that student who best exemplifies the spirit of our school, who has excelled in *all* categories—schol-

147

arship, athletics, student government, extracurricular activities. The faculty was unanimous in selecting this year's recipient: Nina McKenzie."

Nina was startled by the heartfelt applause. All day she'd been afraid of this happening. The truth was she didn't want the award. It only reminded her of the old Nina. She worked her way down the crowded aisle and moved in a trance to the stage. In a strange voice she thanked the faculty for this great honor, and said how special her three years had been. The applause followed her back to her seat, where she studied the handsome plaque. As much as she wanted to disown it, she couldn't help feeling proud.

When the assembly was over, Nina promised Melanie she'd see her tonight. It was the eve of her eighteenth birthday, and Melanie said she had a surprise announcement for the occasion. Nina smiled at her friend's drama and drifted outside.

"Congratulations," a voice stopped her. She knew it was Billy even before she turned, and she didn't resist when he put his arms around her. It felt nice, she had to admit. "That's some honor," he said.

"Thanks."

"How have you been?" he asked.

She could tell he felt awkward. So did she. "Okay, I guess. You?"

He hesitated, shoveling his hands in his jeans. "I was wondering if we could talk. There's something I want to say. It won't take long."

They sat on a bench, ignoring the passing stares. Billy tapped his foot nervously. "I want you to know I still love you," he spoke up. Nina glanced away. Like the award, she really hadn't wanted this, but now that it was offered, it was hard to reject outright.

"What about Donna?"

"I like her. She's fun. But to be honest, I wish it were you I was taking to the prom tonight."

"I'm not going to the prom at all," Nina admitted. "Several boys asked me, but I said no."

"Why?"

"Because it doesn't seem that important to me."

Billy looked frustrated, as if he couldn't believe this was Nina. "The guy from the Army, is he why you don't care about school and me anymore?"

"Not really."

"But you like him?"

"I like him a lot."

"How's he feel about you?"

"Right now he's going through some rough times, and I don't think he's himself. Honestly, I don't know what he thinks about me."

"After we broke up," Billy admitted, "I kept wondering if you thought somehow I wasn't patriotic. That I don't plan to go into the Army doesn't mean I don't love my country. Being a farmer is patriotic, too."

Billy was grasping at straws, Nina saw. When she'd rejected him it was only partly because of Cliff, but Billy would never understand. He was lost without her, she saw now, and suddenly she couldn't help feeling for him. Nina let him take her hand.

"Would you like to get back together?" he asked.

"Billy, I can't."

"Won't you even think about it?"

"I have thought about it."

"But not a lot . . ."

She was quiet, then said, "You know I'm sorry for what happened between us. I shouldn't have done it the way I did."

"It's okay. I forgive you."

Billy was so sincere, she marveled. And she knew now that he'd always be crazy about her, even if they fought. But she didn't want to be his because it was easy. She needed to really care and she didn't love him the way he loved her.

"Can I see you tonight?" he asked. "After the prom?"

"I'm going out with Melanie."

"But afterward. I could come over to your place."

"All right," she said. "But you probably won't want to then."

"I'll be there by eleven. I've really missed you, Nina."

She smiled sadly and hurried off to class. Had she done the right thing to say he could come over? Her parents were going out for the evening, so she could talk privately to Billy. But what was she going to say? The more she was with Billy, the more her resistance got worn down. It seemed like a conspiracy—her parents, the school award, now Billy. The door to forgiveness and reconciliation had been magically opened. All she had to do was step through it.

"Don't be back too late," her mother called from the kitchen as Nina tucked the car keys into her jacket.

Nina felt self-conscious in her jeans and T-shirt

when she knew her friends were all dressed up for the prom. She and Melanie were probably the only hold-outs in their class. Though she wouldn't say it, her mother was upset with Nina for missing a senior prom, as if she were denying herself one of life's great pleasures.

"It's only a dance, Mom," Nina said, peeking into the kitchen. "Not the end of Western civilization."

"I guess not," she admitted, looking a little wistful. "I love to dance."

"Really? You and Dad never go dancing."

"After your father hurt his leg, we never got around to it."

"Bye, Mom," Nina said, and gave her a kiss. Driving to Melanie's, she thought again how little she knew about her parents, especially her mother. Devoted wife, conscientious worker, good bridge partner, avid fiction reader. She and Nina had lived under the same roof for seventeen years, yet her mother had rarely confided in Nina anything that was personal or intimate. It didn't seem fair; Nina had always confided in her. A high school yearbook photo testified that Emily Frazier had been a real looker—what else was there to know? Nina felt that she had a right to know more. Even when she arrived at Melanie's, gingerly pulling out the chocolate cake she'd baked, Nina's thoughts were still on her mother.

"Ta-tum," Nina sang, holding out the cake as Melanie opened the door and her eyes swam to the frosted letters.

HAPPY BIRTHDAY, MELANIE
NO GUTS, NO GLORY!

"You're terrific," Melanie gushed, putting the cake down. "You're a real friend. I wouldn't have survived Castroville without you." She gave Nina a hug.

"How's it feel officially to be an adult? You look terrific with that haircut and earrings."

"I feel like I own the world. Like my life is just beginning."

Melanie's finger took a swipe of the icing. "Not only are you a brain, Nina, you can cook, too. Let's have a piece right now."

While Melanie ducked into the kitchen, Nina roamed the simple house. There wasn't much furniture, and most of it was secondhand. Nina said hello to Melanie's mother, who was watching television in her bedroom. On a hallway table Nina saw a vase of yellow roses. They were magnificent, the most beautiful thing in the house. Before Nina looked at the card she guessed who they were from. She remembered when Billy had used to send her flowers.

"B.J. sent them," Melanie confirmed, looking over Nina's shoulder. "In his birthday card he said he had to go in hock to do it."

"He's really thoughtful."

"I've got something to tell you! Right now. Sit down." An exuberant Melanie thrust a piece of cake at Nina, then popped a split of champagne. "A toast," she declared as she poured the bubbly. The girls clinked glasses. "To B.J. and me!"

"What's going on?" asked Nina, excited.

"A lot."

"Well, are you going to tell me?"

"Of course I'll tell you." She raised her glass again. "B.J. and I are getting married!"

Nina couldn't respond. She'd expected something wild all right, but not this bombshell.

"What's the matter?" asked Melanie.

"Nothing. Everything. Congratulations."

"You don't sound enthusiastic."

"I'm guess I'm a little shocked."

"You're just jealous," Melanie said bluntly, and looked away in disappointment. "Just because things didn't work out between you and Billy—"

"That's not it. I'm just on edge about a lot of things."

"Then you think I'm being rash, don't you?" Melanie said knowingly, though the happiness in her eyes shone through.

"Well, it does seem a little sudden. You haven't known B.J. very long."

"You sound like my mother. She thinks I'm the type who has to learn by making mistakes. Do you think getting married is a mistake? I'm in love. We're in love."

"When did B.J. ask you?"

"He didn't," Melanie said carefully. "I sort of suggested it to him. He's unhappy in the Army, and this is a way out. What's wrong with that?" she asked.

Melanie was defensive. Nina tried to be diplomatic. She knew how sensitive her friend was. "Nothing, if that's what both of you want."

"It's what I want. Actually, B.J. is still thinking about it," she admitted. "We've spoken on the phone a couple of times since I last sneaked on post. In two days he graduates from basic—that's when we're going to set a date."

Nina saw a flicker of anxiety in Melanie's eyes, but

153

it was brushed aside in another toast to the future. She and B.J. would go to New York for their honeymoon, Melanie said blithely, work to save some money, then travel to Europe. The world was their oyster.

There were more toasts until the champagne ran out. Nina asked what the birthday girl wanted to do tonight.

"*Casablanca* is playing in Carmel."

"Sounds great." But Nina couldn't quite match Melanie's exuberant mood. All through the movie, while Melanie sighed over Humphrey Bogart, Nina kept thinking about her future. Melanie, rash or not, now knew exactly what she wanted in life—why didn't Nina know anymore?

"I better get home," Nina said when they walked out of the theater.

"It's only ten."

"I know. I'm sorry. I'm just tired."

She dropped Melanie off without saying a word about tonight's rendezvous with Billy. Her thoughts kept returning to him and made her nervous. She was afraid of making the wrong decision. At home she fixed coffee and tried to sort out her feelings. In the living room she noticed an old photo of her mother— a black-and-white glossy of Emily Frazier as a Castroville High senior. Nina picked it up, hoping i would reveal something, but what she was looking fo didn't materialize. She drifted into her parents' bed room. She knew what she was doing was not exactl proper, but she had to do it.

In the back of her mother's closet she found a must cardboard box that she remembered from years be

re. Her hand dug through the contents. Grade
hool report cards. Brownie scrapbooks. A bap-
smal certification from the First Methodist Church
 Castroville. Buried at the bottom, clamped with a
 bber band, was a file marked HIGH SCHOOL. More
 otos tumbled out along with admiring notes from
 achers and counselors. Love letters from Nina's fa-
 er, too. Nina went through everything. Piece by
 ece, the mosaic came together. She was stunned.
 er mother and father had gone together since their
 phomore year—just like her and Billy. And her
 other had been an honors student: president of her
 nior class . . . an almost straight-A student . . . a
 nalist in scholarship competition. Why hadn't she
 er mentioned these things to Nina? Was her mother
 nbarrassed because all her achievements held
 omise of a great future that had never mate-
 alized? Nina was a carbon copy of her mother, girl
 onder, primed for more success. Yet when Emily
 arried the local boy of her dreams the rainbow
 ded. After Nina's father had shattered his hip in the
 r accident, her mother was forced to drop out of
 llege. The pieces never got put back together. Nina
 ew her mother hadn't finished college but she
 ver realized how much her mother had given up.
 nen Nina came along. Hope was reborn. She was her
 other's second chance. Carefully, Nina put the
 emorabilia back in the box. A second chance for
 hat? To have what happened to her mother happen
  her?
The doorbell rang.
Billy was still in his tux. In his hand was a box of
 ocolates. He tried to act relaxed.

155

"How was it?" Nina asked after she'd poured coffee and they settled in the living room.

"Okay. A great band. I told Donna I didn't want to party."

She listened as he described the evening. "Sounds like I missed something," she said.

Billy couldn't hold his smile. "I don't think so. It was me who missed out by not being with you."

She could feel his hope.

"I don't know why we're making small talk," he said, looking at her. "Nina, I want to get back together."

She expected her stomach to erupt with butterflies but she had never been calmer or more sure of herself. "I can't do that, Billy."

He looked pained. "Why not?"

"Please don't think I'm being cruel to you, but want to be on my own."

"Why? What's independence going to prove? think you're independent enough."

"Billy, haven't you ever wanted to be different from your parents?"

He didn't have to think. "Why should I? My dad' got the best farm in the community. He's always bee prosperous. When I take it over, I'll be prosperou too."

"But haven't you ever wanted to do something o your own, set your own goals, be your own person—

"No," he said honestly.

"But I do."

"I don't get it, Nina."

"I want to leave this town," she explained. "Ther are people here I love very much, like you, people I' always remember. But I know it's time to say good-bye soon."

Helpless, Billy pulled his glance away in surrender. He seemed to know more arguing was pointless. He gave Nina a hug and said quietly, "Then this is it forever." She watched him march out the door, out of her life. It was finally over. Poor Billy would never totally understand.

Alone, Nina drifted out to the porch. The neighborhood was quiet as usual. She felt sad and empty at first. Nothing would ever be the same again, she knew. But maybe that would be all right. With Billy life had been predictable and she'd felt resignation. There was no point in being afraid of the future. She didn't have to live with lukewarm feelings her entire life. Change didn't mean unhappiness, she thought, it meant opportunity.

19

B.J. walked uneasily out of brigade headquarters and hoped for the best. Cliff was still inside. For the last hour the two had sat in the cheerless office of Colonel Donelson, the brigade CO answering questions about Cliff's assault on Bradshaw. The sergeant had been unconscious for thirteen hours, and was covered with cuts and bruises. With a temper like that, Donelson pointed out, maybe Cliff wasn't emotionally or morally fit to be in the United States Army. The irony outraged B.J., but all he could do as a witness was tell of Bradshaw's eight-week campaign of terror. An Army attorney from the adjutant general's staff had accompanied Cliff to the hearing, admitting to the assault but claiming extenuating circumstances. Bradshaw had provoked Cliff deliberately, and with malice. Colonel Donelson, a pensive man with gray-flecked hair and a trim mustache, had listened carefully, taking notes on a yellow legal pad. No trainee in th

158

company came forward to testify for Cliff, except for B.J. Were they all afraid of repercussions from Bradshaw? Cliff told B.J. he felt deserted.

A breeze suddenly broke the stillness of the morning, carrying the sound of the Fort Ord band as it practiced on the parade grounds. The tubas boomed out their notes of triumph. It was still difficult for B.J. to believe, after the grueling weeks, that graduation ceremonies were tomorrow, and even more incredible that he was graduating. He'd made it. No more failure. All he wanted now was for Cliff to be at his side.

The headquarters door creaked open. B.J. tried to anticipate but Cliff's stoical face was unreadable. He looked handsome in his dress greens, stretching his neck up to the sun, as if in reprieve from the gloomy inquisition. Cliff took off his hat and focused on B.J.

"I'm being discharged," he said quietly.

"No—"

"I'm out of the Army for good."

He couldn't believe how calm Cliff was. B.J. turned away in disgust, wanting to hit something. "How could they do that?" he demanded.

"Simple. Army regs." Cliff gazed toward the parade grounds, listening to the band for a moment. "Colonel Donelson was sympathetic, but what it came down to was the regulations. You can't hit your drill sergeant with impunity."

It was all wrong, thought B.J. Regulations were one thing, justice something else. And what about the great soldier Cliff would have made? In its institutional blindness the Army couldn't spot the brilliance of a single individual.

"You can appeal," B.J. said.

"The AG attorney said it would just be wheel-spinning. Once the brigade passes judgment, no other military tribunal is going to presume to know more or better."

"Aren't you angry?"

"I was a few minutes ago," Cliff replied calmly. "I guess the Army isn't always fair. Life isn't fair. I should already have known that. All I had to do was look at my father . . . You know what 'friendly fire' is?" Cliff asked, his face turning subdued. "That's what the Army says if you're killed by your own troops. Friendly fire. It was how my dad was killed. He had radioed in an artillery strike on an enemy position, but the artillery captain miscalculated his coordinates . . ."

"I'm sorry," was all B.J. could say. He was sorry for Cliff, sorry for ever suggesting that he take B.J. with him on the pass, sorry that Bradshaw had gotten away with all this.

"I never thought this would happen," Cliff spoke up. "I always thought I could pull it out."

A switch suddenly clicked in B.J.'s head. He looked at Cliff. "What did you mean when you said that Colonel Donelson was sympathetic to you?"

"What difference does it make?"

"It's important," B.J. insisted.

"He said in the past other trainees have complained about Bradshaw. There have been some investigations, but nothing was substantiated. His fellow sergeants aren't going to rat on him. And no superior officer has ever seen him hit a trainee."

"Not yet anyway."

"What do you mean?"

"It means the war isn't over," B.J. promised. "I've got a plan. It might not get you back in the Army, but it's something we have to do. Remember when you said that the rest of the Army should know about Bradshaw, too?"

B.J. waited until night before he left the barracks and drifted toward the NCO quarters. No one would miss him. A few trainees had sneaked in beer and the platoon would be celebrating half the night. Bradshaw wouldn't be a problem either, because as duty NCO he was isolated in company headquarters. Entering the NCO barracks, B.J. strolled confidently down the hallway as if he lived there. Compared to trainee barracks the accommodations were like the Hilton. Radios blared and voices laughed from behind half-open doors, but no one saw B.J. take a pocketknife and jimmy the flimsy lock on Bradshaw's room. The place was a pig pen, except for one dresser drawer where everything was immaculately clean and well-preserved. B.J. donned the football jersey, pants, helmet, even the socks embossed with Bradshaw's high school logo.

He made one stop before arriving at company headquarters, smearing mud on the jerseys and pants, and knocked on Bradshaw's door.

"Hi there, Sarge," B.J. called, giving an affable nod as he entered. "I was wondering if you'd like to toss around the old ball?"

Bradshaw stared at the defiled uniform. His face crimsoned over.

"What in the hell do you think you're doing, Gibbons?" He rose from behind his desk in cold fury.

"Nothing, Sergeant. I just felt like tossing around a football. Do you like the uniform?"

Bradshaw leaped at him and shoved him against the wall.

"You're not going to hit me *again*, are you, Sergeant?"

"What I did to you before is going to seem like pattycake."

B.J. managed a vindictive smile before the sergeant grabbed him around the neck and slammed him to the floor. Bradshaw got in two quick punches but B.J. felt no pain or distress. The door pushed open. Colonel Donelson and two majors pulled Bradshaw off and stood him up.

"What do you think you're doing, Sergeant?" the colonel demanded.

It took Bradshaw a moment to recover. Still, he didn't understand. "Sir, this man's wearing my clothes—"

"That's not provocation to assault a trainee."

"I didn't know they were the sergeant's," B.J. said innocently. "I found them in the other room, crumpled on the floor, where the rifles are usually kept, sir."

Bradshaw pushed B.J. aside and stormed into the outer office. The padlock on the rifle case was missing, along with the dozen M-16s that belonged to the training cadre.

"Where are the rifles, Sergeant?" Colonel Donelson asked. "You're on duty tonight—"

"This trainee took them . . ."

"I did not, sir."

"Sergeant, you report to my office at oh seven hundred tomorrow."

"Sir, Private Gibbons is trying to make me a scapegoat . . ."

"A private picking on his sergeant?"

"He's trying to ruin my career."

"Sergeant Bradshaw," the colonel said coolly, "I think I should inform you that you may not have a career."

B.J. ducked out with the officers, not looking back. He had no trouble visualizing Bradshaw's fallen face. He couldn't wait to tell Cliff. He didn't feel one bit guilty. After all, he thought, an eye for an eye.

20

Melanie hooked her arm through B.J.'s as they mingled with other trainees and their families on the parade grounds, waiting for the graduation ceremonies to begin. The band anchored one corner of the field, near the bleachers, which were starting to fill, and a color guard stood on another, tall and erect with white gloves and brass buttons that gleamed in the sunlight. Melanie gave B.J. another kiss on the cheek. "How do I look?" she asked.

"Just great," said B.J. admiringly.

She had gone on a shopping spree in Carmel—this was a special occasion. The only graduation ceremony she was going to attend. She'd decided to forsake her high school's because her three years had been practically meaningless. When B.J. was free, so would she be.

"What's the matter?" Melanie asked. "You're sc quiet."

"Nothing."

"You're nervous, too . . ."

"Really?"

"Come on . . ."

"Okay." He faced her, looking pensive. "I guess we have to talk."

"I know we do. About when we're getting married, where we're going to live, what we'll do for money . . ."

"I don't mean that," he said.

She felt her stomach tighten.

"Melanie, you know how I feel about you. And I owe you a lot. But I've done a lot of thinking . . ."

B.J. stopped himself, afraid to hurt her. A lot had happened in eight weeks. He recognized clearly now why he had joined the Army. He'd been running away from his problems, and from himself. Cliff had seen that in him a long time ago. And when B.J. told Melanie in desperation that if he could only be free again he'd find his niche, it was just more running. It was time to stop, to leave school and his old success behind, to earn his pride all over again. He wasn't exactly in love with the military but he'd learned to respect it—along with his place in it. There were narrow limits here, but it was the limits that forced him to look at himself without blinking.

"You don't want to get married, do you?" she spoke for him.

"I just can't," he admitted.

The pain churned up from her stomach. "Why? What's wrong? Is it that I'm not pretty enough, or funny, or I act too romantic—"

"Nothing is *wrong*. You're wonderful."

She didn't believe him.

"Melanie, don't look at me like that, please. I love you. It's just that marriage isn't right for me. At least not now."

A chill feathered over her. Why was this happening? How was it happening to her? She didn't deserve it, not after how much she'd helped B.J. Did he know how much courage it had taken her to ask him to marry her?

"I've learned a lot in the Army," he said simply. "One thing I've learned is that I'm too young to get married."

B.J. suddenly seemed remote and inflexible, as if nothing would convince him otherwise. Didn't he know how she felt? Anger mixed with her panic. "B.J., I told Nina we were getting married. I told my best friend."

"Please forgive me, Melanie," he said.

She dropped her head on his shoulder and started to cry. "Don't do this to me, B.J. Please marry me."

"I can't. Maybe someday—"

"No, now," she said, her voice catching. "I'm so tired of being disappointed."

B.J. took her gently by the shoulders. "Melanie, you have to accept this."

"I don't want to accept it! I may act strong, but I'm really not. I need somebody. I need you."

B.J. tried to console her but she pulled back, finding her composure. Walking back to her car, she waited for B.J. to come after her. When he saw that she could be independent and determined he would change his mind. He would respect her. She felt sure. But with each step her hope faded a little more, and when she reached her car she heard only a military march with trumpets and trombones blaring across the open sky.

21

The packed cardboard boxes were strewn haphazardly across Melanie's living room like an obstacle course. She finished stuffing another carton with books and, struggling to keep the flaps down, taped it shut. Nina helped her squeeze pots and pans into still another.

"Your mom doesn't mind your taking some kitchen stuff?" Nina asked.

"She insists," said Melanie. "Being on my own is the only way I'll come to my senses, she says, but she wants to help out all she can."

"She'll miss you a lot, I bet," Nina said. "Just like me."

"I'll miss you, too. But you know I've got to get out of this place." She laughed. "I'd be the world's biggest hypocrite if I didn't."

Her thoughts shifted to B.J. for a moment. She wondered how much she'd miss him. After leaving the graduation ceremonies, she had cried enough tears to fill a swimming pool. Then at the bank she'd withdrawn a big chunk of her savings and spent a weekend in San Francisco on a binge of self-indulgence unknown in the annals of Castroville. She put herself up at an expensive hotel, went to the theater both nights, and did plenty of shopping. Several boys had tried to pick her up, but she refused. She wanted to prove she could be independent. But driving home, putting everything in perspective, she knew that she didn't need to prove anything. She was what she was. She didn't hate herself or want to self-destruct. She liked herself. She had exposed her soul to B.J. and he'd rejected her—but it was because of himself that he'd said no, not because of her. Her spirits found a way to rebound. She was still going to New York to find her fame and fortune.

Melanie finished folding some sweaters in a carton laced with mothballs, then stared at the envelope she had retrieved from her closet. The picture of the boy from West Point was inside, along with a snapshot of B.J. He'd mailed her a letter and the photo after graduation. His note explained that he was being transferred to Fort Benning in Georgia, without a leave, but he wanted her to know he would write. The letter made Melanie happy. In her heart she forgave B.J. for everything. He was only doing what he had to do. As for the future, she thought, you could never tell.

She stashed the envelope with the clothes.

"I better be off," Nina said when they'd carried all the boxes to the car. She put her hand on Melanie's shoulder. "Are you going to be all right?"

"Don't tell me you're worried? After all I've been through? I'm tough. Didn't you know that?"

"I care about you, that's all. I'm sorry things didn't work out."

"I'll be hunky-dory."

"Have you got a place to stay in New York?"

"For the first couple of weeks. I'll be with the same family I visited a couple of summers ago. They're really understanding. After that I rent an apartment and get a job."

"I'll miss you," Nina said again. "You gave me lot of courage the last few months. You were a bigger help than you know. You promise to write?"

"Promise," Melanie said, and fought back a tear.

They embraced again, and then Melanie wedged herself into the Chevy piled high with boxes. She could barely get the top up. All that was left was to stop for gas, say goodbye to her mom at Burt's Burger Bowl, and hit the road. Free at last. She'd drive three thousand miles to glimpse cities, towns, and people she'd never seen—adventures waiting to happen! Suddenly she couldn't wait. As she'd always told Nina, her life was just beginning. Now she really believed it.

22

Nina sat near the fifty-yard line and gazed wistfully at a field of trampled, balding grass. The school was deserted—summer session didn't begin for another week—and the emptiness felt strange. She half-expected the bleachers to fill momentarily with raucous kids, for Billy to sit next to her, the cheerleaders to strut out. So many memories . . . It had been a great three years, though at graduation she'd felt awkward. Nina's gaze had kept wandering toward her parents. They were smiling but obviously they weren't happy. Her breaking up with Billy and throwing her plans to the wind had broken their hearts. Now they were eager for her to decide what she would do with her life—quickly, as if life were a race with only one route to take. Nina was in no hurry at all. Almost everyone she knew who'd done well at school was ambitious. They couldn't wait to succeed or make a ton of money. They all felt it was expected of them. Nina laughed as she realized she felt different now. It was all one big pressure cooker and she had had enough of that.

As the morning sun warmed her face, she stood up and decided to walk to town just as someone called her name. She focused on the form of a boy in cutoff jeans and a T-shirt. Out of uniform, his face free of bruises, Cliff was hard to recognize. B.J. had confided to Melanie that Cliff had been discharged. Melanie had told Nina. She wrote Cliff a note to say she was sorry and boldly added that she hoped they'd meet again. She pondered her words—especially after what had happened in the mess hall. She'd felt so comfortable with him at one time.

"Hi," she called nervously as he approached.

"Hi," he said, and dug his hands in his pockets. "I stopped by your house. Your mother said you might be hiding out here."

"That must have been interesting," Nina observed. "Mom says I'm hiding out. You know she blames you or Melanie for everything except the Fall of Rome."

"She was civilized to me. She told me where to find you at least."

"You make good first impressions. You did on me anyway."

"Sure," he said, "it was the second that wasn't so great."

"It's okay. Those were rough times for you. I understand what you were going through."

Without even thinking about it, she slipped her arm through Cliff's. It felt natural and they wandered out of the school yard. "I'm really sorry about your discharge. That must have been devastating. It was unfair. I wish I could have helped."

"At first I was stunned, but when I began to think about the eight weeks, I realized that maybe it was inevitable. It's always been hard for me to accept that some things you can't control, like losing my father, like this. Life takes its course whether you like it or not. I didn't die from this. I'm alive and kicking."

"But your dream was to be an officer—"

"I wanted it to be my dream," Cliff corrected. "I believed that's what my dad would have wanted for me. It wasn't necessarily what I wanted. I never asked myself about that. I think I was afraid to find out the answer. If I hadn't been discharged I probably wouldn't have had the courage to quit on my own. I'd have completed the plan without a second thought. I can't say I like what happened, but now I have a chance to figure out what I want for me."

Nina considered her own life and her recent choices. She understood perfectly. "Are you mad at the Army?" she said.

"B.J. and my mother asked the same thing. I'm not holding the entire U.S. Army responsible. There are some great things about the Army. I wanted to serve my country, and I still do. If it won't be in the military, it'll be some other way."

"Like?"

Cliff shrugged, then smiled pensively. "I'd like some time to think everything out. Right now I just want to unwind. I was thinking of moving to San Francisco."

As they walked, Nina talked about her own ups and downs. She and Billy were through, she wasn't going to college right away, she wasn't sure what she would do. And that was fine with her.

"That's pretty bold," Cliff said. "Are you nervous?"

"I'm trying not to be." She glanced at Cliff. "You think I'll be okay?"

"You always had a lot of spirit. That's why you went out with me in the first place, wasn't it? I liked that night," he said, putting an arm around her.

Nina dropped her head on his shoulder. "Me, too. I'd like to go back and dance with you. I won't be mean this time—promise."

"It may sound crazy, but looking back," Cliff said, "our confrontation in the mess hall wasn't so bad. You didn't get upset with me even though I gave you a hard time. You listened. You cared. I never had that with a girl. That's why I wanted to see you again. You're smart and nice—and pretty too."

Suddenly he reached out to her. She let Cliff kiss her. She kissed him back. She realized how much she liked really caring about someone. Not because everyone thought it was a good match, but because the feelings were strong and real. Maybe she needed Cliff in her life. She didn't want to replace Billy with someone new just for the sake of having a boyfriend, but Cliff was different from Billy. He didn't want her to be docile. He would give her all the freedom she wanted. They weren't making any plans. They both had lots to think about.

That was the great thing about the future, Nina thought, relaxing. It wasn't even here yet and anything could happen.

ABOUT THE AUTHOR

MICHAEL FRENCH is a native of Los Angeles who currently lives in Santa Fe, New Mexico, with his wife and their children. Time permitting, he is a serious mountain trekker who favors exotic and remote destinations, among them New Guinea, the Amazon, Java and Rwanda. Michael French is the author of several adult books as well as numerous young adult novels, including *Lifeguards Only Beyond This Point*, *The Throwing Season*, and *Pursuit*, which won the California Young Readers Medal, as well as the Starfire novels, *Circle of Revenge* and *Us Against Them*.